THE HEART
IS ITS
OWN REASON

Natalie C.

THE HEART
IS ITS
OWN REASON

NATALEE CAPLE

INSOMNIAC PRESS

First edition.

This book was written between December 1993 and December 199
This book is a work of fiction.

Edited by Mike O'Connor
Copy edited by Lloyd Davis & Liz Thorpe
Designed by Mike O'Connor

Canadian Cataloguing in Publication Data

Caple, Natalee, 1970-
    The heart is its own reason

ISBN 1-895837-25-1

I. Title.

PS8555.A5583H42 1998   C813'.54   C98-930291-1
PR9199.3.C36H42 1998

The publisher and author gratefully acknowledge the support of th
Ontario Arts Council

Some of these stories have appeared previously in: *Descant, Grain, McGi
Street Magazine, Meow Press Chapbooks, The Capilano Review, The Malaha
Review, The New Quarterly, THIS Magazine,* and *Smoke.*

Printed and bound in Canada

Insomniac Press, 393 Shaw Street,
Toronto, Ontario, Canada, M6J 2X4
www.insomniacpress.com

For Mali Lol and Lesje Serengeti.

The worm is in the man's heart.
That is where it must be sought.

—Albert Camus, *The Myth of Sisyphus*

CONTENTS

For their generous support and assistance I would like to thank: my publisher: Mike O'Connor; my family: Patricia Caple, Russell Caple, and Suzanne Caple; my teachers: Valerie Copeland, Christopher Dewdney, and Michael Stubitsch; and my friends: Christian Bök, Katy Chan, Bonnie Halverson, Nick Kazamia, Karen Mac Cormack, Brian Panhuyzen, Kelly Ryan, Alan Tomassini, and Darren Wershler-Henry.

Special thanks to Natalie Panhuyzen for providing specific medical information for some of these stories.

—Natalee Caple

THE
PRICE
OF ACORN

Acorn's mother was sixteen when she married the only boy she had ever been familiar with. It was a very windy day. The church was being renovated and so the back wall was only half there. The wind whistled into the church through that hole and chased around the wedding party like a frantic dog. Acorn's mother held her skirt down with one hand and her veil on with the other.

When the priest asked if she did, she screamed, "What?"

"Do you take this man to be your lawfully wedded husband?" the priest shouted back.

"Tell him yes!" her mother yelled from behind her.

"Yes," Acorn's mother yelled, although she truly did not know what she was agreeing to.

After the final words Acorn's father swept his adolescent bride up in his big, policeman arms and tried to carry her out of the church archway for the photographer. In the pictures they are both scrunching their faces up and lurching wildly forward into the wind.

They didn't make love the first night. As soon as the lights were out they fell asleep, their hands frozen as they moved toward their nuptial goals. Once, in the night, Acorn's father woke feeling uneasy. His wife was leaning over him, completely asleep, but staring. Her huge eyes trying to place him, this man in her bed.

"Delia, honey, it's all right," he told her, holding up his ringed finger for her to see. Slowly, she lay back into the wiry mattress. He rolled onto his side to look at her. She was so tiny, two feet shorter than him, and with a waist no thicker than his leg. Her breaths were deep and hiccupy. She slept like a distressed child.

Her tossing had caused her nightgown to ride up over her hips. The modest white cotton panties covered her to the waist. The band was just a little frayed, rising and falling. Her hipbones beneath his thumbs reminded him of the shoulders of a bird and he thought to himself, What if I let her go and these hips began to rise and move and then just flew away? How would I explain that?

Softly, not wanting to wake her, he traced the outside of her bright, firm, little breast with his forefinger. He moved the finger across her breast toward the middle of her chest. He thought that her heart would be there. He kept moving down the front of her nightgown, over the ribbon and shirring. He watched her face carefully to see if she was waking. She was fast asleep. He reached the thin, elastic waistband and he stopped to make sure that she was absolutely asleep. Hooking the elastic carefully with his finger he passed his hand down toward her softness. He brushed the wiry hair quickly and dove deeper. Slightly careless with excitement, he had to knock her legs further apart. And what did he find? She was wet already. Her warmth reminded him of the swimming pond after a hot day, when the night air is cooler than the water.

Acorn's mother was dreaming as she lay there. She was dreaming that she was sitting in her grandmother's red velvet chair, drinking tea out of the old china with the fruit pattern. And as she sat there the wooden arms of the chair came alive, became adventurous with her. The bulbs at the end of the arms sprouted fingers that touched her and entered her. She felt guilty because she had saved herself so completely for so long only to be taken advantage of on her wedding night by her grandmother's chair.

Acorn's parents kept these first touches secret from each other for the whole of their marriage.

Acorn's father was named Kimberly. Kimberly being a difficult name for a man and Kim being equally traumatic he was referred to most often as Burly. It suited him. Burly had to duck in every doorway. His policeman's uniform had to be specially made for him and his belts were almost as long as Delia when she lay on the floor.

Big as he was, when Delia became pregnant with Acorn it was Burly's giant ankles which swelled out of his boots. It was Burly who couldn't sleep on his stomach and it was Burly who suddenly changed all of his nutritional desires. Delia took care of him with the sweetest of sympathy right up until her water broke. When her water broke she lost all her confidence.

Burly took charge. He carried Delia to the truck and laid her down on a mattress he had tied in the back. He wedged her in place with two dressers and then lined the sides of the dressers with pillows so that she would be comfortable. It was a half-hour drive to the hospital. He kept the little window behind the driver's seat open so he could shout to her as he drove and make sure she was all right. She cried for the first ten minutes and then she was quiet. When Burly finally pulled into the hospital parking lot and jumped out to retrieve his wife he found that somehow she had managed to fall asleep. The back of his truck had been transformed into a giant crib.

Delia slept through the entire delivery. The doctor kept asking what kind of drugs she had taken but Burly insisted that Delia had never even taken an aspirin in her life. Her body was responsive even if she was unconscious and Acorn was born easily.

When she woke up she was in a maternity bed. There was no one else in the room and the sun was setting bright red in the middle of the window that her bed was pushed up to.

"Hello? Hello?" she called. "Burly? Hello?"

What if they don't know I'm pregnant? she thought. What if I rolled out of the truck and had the baby on the dirt road while Burly drove on thinking that he had me and the baby rolled down a hill and the first person who came by only saw me?

"Hello, somebody? Burly?"

Burly had been down the hall talking to the doctor. When they heard Delia's weak voice calling they walked together to her room. On the way they asked a nurse to go and get the baby.

"Delia, honey," Burly said as he sat down beside her on the bed and smoothed her fine blonde hair from her sweaty forehead. "We had a boy."

Delia looked into his eyes bewildered and asked him, "When? When did we have a boy?"

The nurse cleared her throat at the door. In her arms was something blue and lumpy. She walked forward, smiling at Delia. Delia opened her arms and accepted the bundle warily. As she looked down she saw that it was true; they had a boy.

"How long was I asleep?"

"You were asleep for a whole day," the nurse answered. "You should feed him now."

Delia looked up at her with such concern that the nurse began to coo comfortingly.

"But I don't know how," Delia cried.

With the nurse's guidance Delia shrugged out of her nightgown and adjusting her hold on the new baby, he was brought to her breast. He seemed to know what she didn't. Burly watched them and didn't say anything until his son began to suckle. Then he leaned over and put his finger on the top of Delia's nipple just above his son's mouth and he said, "It looks like two acorns kissing."

Acorn had a healthy infancy and grew into an iron-limbed toddler. He broke everything that could be broken. Whenever a visiting family member would think they spotted something still in one piece they would immediately pick it up to see where it had been glued. Acorn learned to use a walker and he tore around the house like he was being chased by demons.

One day Delia and Burly decided that a bed and breakfast would bring in the extra money that they needed now that Acorn was off the breast. The back bedroom was finished and an ad was placed. Two weeks later they had their first and only visitor.

🍂

Delia is talking to her mother on the phone. She is sitting, looking out the kitchen window and she sees someone walking up to the house. Acorn is lying across the front of her calves, clinging like a squirrel to a tree and Delia swings him gently up and down.

As the man gets closer to the house she describes him to her mother, "He's a lot shorter than Burly and pretty old. I think he might be sixty or seventy even. He's got a small, green suitcase and a tweed jacket over his arm. He's got a black leather briefcase, too. He's limping. I better go and help him, Mom. I'll call you later." Delia hangs up and scooping Acorn up to her shoulder she runs to the front door.

When she opens the door he is standing there. He is leaning against the door frame wiping his soaking face with a handkerchief. His eyes, when he looks at her, are red veined and watery.

"This is the bed and breakfast," he says.

"Yes," Delia answers, feeling a little embarrassed.

"I'll be staying for a week," he tells her.

"How old are you?" Delia blurts out.

He shakes his head and puts a finger in his ear before he answers her, "I'm fifty-two. How old are you, if I may ask?"

Delia grins happily and shifting Acorn to her hip, she answers, "I'm eighteen." Nodding to Acorn, "He's two and a bit."

Adderly Brown calls himself an academic. He laughs for them when he says it. Burly is home and Acorn is asleep in his lap as they eat at the dinner table.

"I'm giving a lecture at the university. I am going to be discussing how film would have developed if sound hadn't been invented when it was." Adderly laughs when he says this.

Burly laughs too and tries to play along by saying, "I didn't even know sound was invented. I thought it was always there."

Adderly gives Burly a peculiar look and Delia rushes to laugh at Burly's joke.

"I just finished a speaking engagement in Barcelona. It was beastly hot. I'm sure you have noticed the sunburn on my ample scalp." Adderly laughs at himself again.

Burly stirs his potatoes with his fork and says humourlessly, "Yes, I had noticed that."

Delia's plate is empty. Being nervous about her guest, she ate her dinner at breakneck speed. Her stomach is still rumbling because it doesn't yet realize how full she is. She tries to muffle the noise with her napkin. Adderly ate his asparagus and the bread but he appears to be finished now, even though his mashed potatoes and his pork chop are untouched.

He sees Delia staring at his plate and he explains, "I'm a vegetarian. I'm sorry, I should have told you. I don't eat meat or dairy products because I have a terrible fear of death." He laughs.

"Excuse me?" Delia doesn't understand what he means about death.

"Oh, I was joking, my dear. I don't eat meat because I believe we are capable of finding alternative sources of protein without taking advantage of other life forms."

Burly has taken his pork chop up in his hand and is tearing off the meat with his lips held back to show his teeth. He waves the half-devoured meat at Adderly and says, "You eat fish?"

"Yes," answers Adderly, as if he does not see where this is going.

"What's your favourite movie?" Delia dashes brightly in.

"Fish is meat. Meat is muscle," Burly says darkly and

continues, "Plants are life forms too. The way I see it, the first thing you have to do if you're going to be moral about eating is start ranking the life forms. But I guess you would know what order they go in."

Burly throws his pork chop down and hands Acorn over to Delia. He doesn't excuse himself. He just stomps upstairs without even pushing his chair back in. Delia looks at Adderly and smiles awkwardly.

"My favourite movie is *Harvey*."

Adderley purses his lips and squints his eyes. "The giant, invisible rabbit movie? With James Stewart, I believe. Why is that your favourite movie then, Delia?"

"I think it's funny."

Adderly laughs nastily at this. When he stops laughing he gives Delia an assessing look. Then he looks at Acorn who is playing with the buttons on the bodice of her dress.

"May I see him?" Adderly asks and reaches forward to take Acorn out of her arms. He lifts Acorn under the arms and holds him away so that he can look at him. He turns Acorn around and examines him as if he were a cat in a cat show. Acorn is quite heavy so he gives him back. Acorn does not like being handled so.

"Do you have any children?" Delia asks, rubbing Acorn's back briskly to soothe him.

"None of my own, no," Adderly responds. He continues to stare at Acorn.

For the next few days Adderly stays around the house. He is preparing his lecture. Burly stays away from him but Delia and Acorn find him curious.

"You know, Delia, your boy is quite amazing. He really is quite advanced for his age," Adderly says, examining the red and blue crayon scribble that Acorn has made on the table around his coffee cup. Delia flushes with pleasure and looks at her son.

"Do you think so?" she asks. Adderly praises Acorn often. It confirms for Delia her suspicion that her child is unusually talented.

"Yes, I do think so. Strange, considering his father. You haven't arranged school for him yet?"

"Oh, no," Delia answers. She is ironing. "He's not even three yet."

"Well, this is a heightened learning time for him. I don't suppose you even have a decent Montessori here, do you?" Adderly sighs deeply. "I hate to see it."

Delia sets the iron down and looks at Acorn counting his toes on the floor.

"I don't know what you mean, Adderly. What's a Montessori?"

Adderly is happy to have the floor.

"A Montessori, my dear, is a place where very young children of exceptional abilities are stimulated to learn. A child like yours will never develop in an ordinary environment. Acorn could easily be a future Glenn Gould or Roman Polanski. But, I'm afraid that if he's left to the public system he is likely to become another flatfoot like Burly."

"I heard that," calls Burly from the front door. He strides in with only a few swings of his long legs. He grabs Acorn from the ground and swings him over his shoulders. Acorn shrieks happily.

"He already has flat feet, don't you, son?" jokes Burly and he chews mockingly on one of Acorn's bare heels as Acorn wriggles and laughs and slaps Burly's back.

"Me and my boy are going to get us some dairy ice cream in town. Are you coming, wife?" Without waiting for her answer Burly bends down and unplugs the iron. As he straightens he knocks Delia on to his other shoulder and she shrieks along with Acorn as he carries them to the truck.

They get free ice cream because Burly is a cop. They sit in the truck licking the creamy stuff. Burly has chocolate, Acorn has tiger tail, Delia has strawberry cheesecake. Acorn's face is covered with sticky orangeness. He kicks his feet against the dashboard as he sits between them.

"Ti-gah, Ti-gah," he says.

Delia looks at Burly. Burly is staring out the windshield at the people who come out of the ice cream shop into the parking lot. He makes Adderly look small and stooped. Burly's face and neck are tanned and his black hair is cropped so short that she can see the white scalp underneath. Burly has a big clean jaw. He eats his ice cream seriously.

Acorn is now crawling on the truck floor by her feet. He is trying to wedge his whole body into the corner. Delia reaches her arm across to tug on Burly's blue collar.

"I think you're jealous of my spending so much time with Adderly."

Burly laughs and pats his crotch. "I know something about academics you don't," he says.

That night Delia gets out of bed because she hears Acorn fretting. She opens the door to her bedroom and looks down the hall. She sees Adderly in his pyjamas, standing by Acorn's door, looking in on him.

"Delia, let me come right out and say it. My lecture is tomorrow and I'll be leaving from the university. I want to take Acorn with me."

Delia is up to her elbows in the dishes.

"What?" she says.

Adderly is standing behind her. He moves to hand her one of the plates that are piled up beside the sink.

"I want to take Acorn with me. I have already told you what a special boy he is. If you let me take him, he will live with me and be under my supervision. I will make sure that he is properly trained to the best of his abilities. You will, of course, see him frequently. I will happily pay all of your travel expenses."

Delia stares at the cups under the water and tries to think.

"Where do you live?" she asks.

Adderly laughs.

"I live in Toronto," he answers indulgently. "You could drive there in less than three hours."

The doorbell rings. Delia shakes the soap off of her gloves and goes to answer it. At the door is a delivery man with an enormous cardboard box on a metal cart.

"I didn't order anything," she tells the teenage boy who is offering her a clipboard and pen.

"I did," says Adderly, coming from behind her. He takes the clipboard and putting a hand on Delia's hip, he moves her out of the way and motions the boy to bring the package in.

"Why did he buy us a washing machine?"

"Shh, keep your voice down."

Delia and Burly are in bed.

"He wants it to be nice for Acorn when he comes home. He says it will keep his clothes cleaner."

"I didn't say he could go, and you're already talking about when he comes back." Burly rolls onto his stomach. The pillow is bunched up in his arms and he is propping his chin up on it. Delia doesn't wear her nightgown when it's this hot. She shimmies up beside him.

"Don't you want the best for Acorn? Adderly says if we just let him go for a few months it will make a big difference. I love you, Burly. But I want Acorn to be something special."

"Cops are special. You tell me who you call when you're in trouble, or when there's a riot, or a natural disaster or something? You don't call an academic, I'll tell you that."

"I know, Burly. I'll tell him no."

Burly is quiet for a long time before he says, "I already told him yes. Do you know what he said when I brought Acorn's bag down? He said he was going to buy Acorn new clothes when they get to Toronto."

"Hush, Burly. Our baby won't be gone long." Delia rolls on top of Burly and begins kissing the back of his neck. When he finally lies flat, releasing the pillow and putting his arms behind him, patting Delia's hips, she presses her face against his shoulder and they fall asleep.

Acorn wasn't fussy, but then he didn't really understand. A taxi came and took them away. Delia and Burly stood in the doorway watching the dust kick up from the wheels. The car was long gone before they turned back to the house. Burly didn't go to work. They spent the rest of the day doing the laundry.

"I've called every day and I keep getting that machine. Why doesn't he answer our calls? I just want to know if Acorn is all right, how he's settling in. It would make Acorn feel better to hear my voice."

"I'm sorry, ma'am. I can't make anyone answer their phone. Perhaps you should be talking to the police?" The operator sounds as if she would like to help.

"No, that's all right. Thank you, but my husband is the police. I'll talk to him when he gets home."

Delia hangs the phone up. She stares at the receiver and twists the fabric of her dress in her lap with nervous hands.

"I don't like the way it bangs around." Burly is in a bad mood. He sits on an orange crate and stares at it shuddering and knocking back and forth. He has put too big of a load in the washing machine again. He looks up at the ceiling to where Delia is standing in the kitchen. He yells, "All my socks are blue!"

It has been a week today and now they are going to Toronto to see Acorn. Burly loads the washing machine onto the back of the truck and Delia sits in the passenger seat with her seat belt already on. As Burly walks around to get in she reaches over and turns the key in the ignition.

When they finally arrive in the city, it takes them awhile to locate Adderly's house. It is right on the water. It is a big house tucked away at the end of a long driveway. It is plain-faced and white with dozens of odd-shaped windows on all sides. The hedges by the driveway are trimmed to resemble tall, slender birds. The doorbell plays a song. Adderly answers the door. He looks agitated.

"Well, Delia, I'm happy to see you. Come in. Acorn's not here right now. He's at school, but come in. Let me show you around."

"I called you every day," Delia says and she pushes him out of the way and marches in, looking around for evidence of Acorn.

"Did you? I must not have a tape in my machine. You're

probably worried. I'm sorry. Why is Burly bringing the machine in?"

Burly has picked the machine up in his arms and carried it into the front hall. When he puts it down the tiles make a serious cracking noise.

"Where's Acorn?" he demands.

"I just finished telling Delia that Acorn is not here."

"He's here," Delia says, "I can smell him."

Adderly controls a laugh.

"Why don't I show you Acorn's room? I'm sure that you would like to see where he's staying. And then I'll show you some of the work we've done."

Adderly begins to walk up the stairs and Delia shoves past him, running. At the top of the stairs are five doors. The first two are locked. The door at the end of the hall is open, she can see that it is the bathroom. The next door opens and it is a child's room.

She walks over to the bed. It is cleanly made. There are toys arranged neatly across the pillow. Delia knocks the toys off and pulls the pillow out and examines it. Adderly comes to the door.

"Everything all right?" he asks. Burly is behind him. There is another door which leads to an adjoining room. Delia runs to it and tears into Adderly's bedroom.

She runs to the king-sized bed and grabs both of the pillows out from under the covers. One of the pillows has a corner which has been savagely chewed.

"Where is he?" she screams as she throws herself against Adderly and knocks his thin body to the floor. "Where is he?"

Burly lifts her off. He grabs Adderly by his silk tie and brings him to his feet and throws him on the bed.

"Go downstairs and wait for me," Burly orders Delia. She hesitates for a moment. She doesn't know what is happening. And then she turns and leaves the room.

Left alone with the rapidly paling Adderly, Burly locks one hand around his throat. He shakes him quickly and then releases him. Coughing and gasping, Adderly regains himself.

"You can't do this, Burly. You are a police officer. You

know this is assault. I'm keeping Acorn here and if you try to do anything about it I'll tell everyone you sold your son to me for a washing machine. I'll say I only took him because I felt for him and I'll show everyone how much better I treat him. I'll show everyone what a stupid and violent man his father is. I may not be bigger than you, Burly, but my lawyers are." Adderly is standing now. His red eyes are burning in his forehead. His bald head is shining like a bulb.

Burly hears something outside of the room, a creak and a click and the sound of Delia's footsteps running down the stairs.

Delia is sitting on the washing machine. Her hands grip the sides of it protectively. She stares up at the ceiling. It's been a long time but now they are coming down.

Adderly walks in front. She is surprised to see that he is not bleeding. Burly walks down behind him. He is slumped. In his hand Delia sees a fan of dollars.

"What's going on? Where's Acorn? Burly, what happened?"

"Get back in the truck, Delia."

Burly is moving toward her. Adderly is smiling. Delia screams and hits Burly in the face. He stumbles but he does not stop. He throws her over his shoulder, still screaming and punching and calling for Acorn. He bends down and picks up the washing machine, pinning her legs to his chest as he holds it. With his knees bent so that they almost break he carries her and the machine back to the truck. Adderly shuts the door the second they are beyond it.

As soon as the door closes Delia is quiet. She lets Burly edge the machine carefully onto the back of the truck and carry her around to the passenger seat. Adderly is looking out the window at them. Delia leans her head against the dashboard and wraps her arms around her belly to control her shaking. Burly is roping the machine in, its new value made obvious by his care.

Burly slips in beside her and she turns her face away from him. He starts the truck. They roll out of the driveway and turn onto the road.

When they round the corner Delia sits up and smoothes her hair.

"It's my birthday next week," she says. Her voice is hoarse. "I'm going to be nineteen."

"Yes," says Burly. He drives around another corner and pulls over by the grassy lawn of a park. He leans to Delia and puts his big hand around the back of her head. He grips her hair. He leans into her face. He kisses her.

"Delia," he says. "Go and get our son out of the washing machine."

THE
TROUBLE
WITH KILLING
SOMEONE YOU KNOW

"This morning, just when I was waking up and your mother was still asleep beside me, I heard you whispering. I heard your voice, I swear it wasn't in my head, saying, 'Do you still think about me?' Yes. Yes, I think about you every time I break a glass, and when the subway train rushes into the station, and when my heart beats, I think about you.

"It's been seven days since I last spoke to my lawyer and he told me that if I don't stop following my brother I will be arrested. So I agreed and then I bought myself a new jacket and a wig. Because they don't know. They don't know what it is to lose your child and to wait for your child to be returned to you and to find your child in a photograph in a courtroom two years later. They don't know or else they would all buy jackets and wigs and walk behind me as I follow him."

"Howard? Howard, are you listening to me?"

Howard Moss is fifty years old. Ten years ago his eight-year-old daughter was kidnapped and beaten to death by his only brother, to whom he was very close. Howard is sitting on the edge of the bathtub running the water for a bath and his wife is talking to him through the locked bathroom door. "Howard, I'm going out to buy the gun now. Do you think you can wait until I get back?" Howard nods his head and she must know this because she picks up her bag and leaves. He can hear her taking her keys out, going downstairs, and the slip of the bolt as she locks the door. Tonight Howard and Helen Moss are going to break into his brother's home and shoot his brother in the head then Howard Moss will shoot his wife in the shoulder and shoot himself in the heart and it will seem as if he lost his mind. Nothing too technical, he just lost his mind.

The walls are beginning to perspire, the wallpaper fretting under the weight of the steam that pours up from the thundering faucet. Howard gets undressed. As he peels the dampened clothes from his body he stares into the gathering steam. It seems to him as if it has begun to thicken and take on shapes. It seems as if his daughter might be somewhere inside the winding grayness and he strains for her.

"Because you had black eyes as shiny and round as wet grapes and your hair was soft and your little arms were round and fat and I carried you everywhere until you were so big it hurt my back and even then for awhile I still carried you. Because I threw out all your drawings thinking that there were too many of them and that there would be too many more. Because your mother wakes up screaming every night and she cries all the time, her face is always swollen and last year I actually punched her for crying. I punched her right in her swollen face. Because we took you camping and you touched the water and it was so marvellously soft that after that you called everything you liked 'soft as lake water'. I don't understand. I'll never understand. And I don't remember him being my brother. I don't remember what I must have felt for him before. I can hardly even remember our parents now, only a tiny echo of my mother's fingers in my hair while I am lying on the counter and the tap is running."

Howard climbs into the tub. Under the water his flesh is paler and flabbier but his body can no longer startle him. He leans back, bending his knees and drawing them out of the water so that he can submerge his shoulders and his neck. He tries to reconstruct his memories, to dig out something about her that isn't covered by her death. But he can't. And it doesn't even matter any more. Greater than any endearing infantile event, greater than the eerie sweetness of her pictures in every room, greater even than her name, is the violent absence of her. For a moment, almost as a reflex, Howard thinks of drowning himself and then he sits up. He hears something downstairs and he thinks that Helen must be back.

"Helen? Helen, did you get it?"

Howard listens but does not hear another sound. He draws himself out of the bath water, and pulls a towel around his waist, having to hold it in place because of his girth. He pushes the bathroom door open and looks down the hall. The house is quiet but there is something, a loud ticking, a familiar, ridiculously loud ticking. His father's pocket watch. Which indicates his brother's pocket.

"Olson?" Howard calls.

"I'm here," he hears his brother's voice answer.

"Olson, how did you get in?" Howard is creeping backwards toward his bedroom and his clothes.

"I forced the basement window. Don't you remember how I would always lose my key and force our parents' basement window?" He sounds so friendly. Howard feels something quiver deep between his ribs and he hopes that Helen arrives soon with the gun. He thinks that he should lock himself in the bathroom again and turn the water back on. That way when she comes home and finds Olson she will shoot him and Howard can pretend that he didn't know yet that his brother was in the house.

"Howard?" Olson hasn't moved from the bottom of the stairs.

"Just let me get dressed and I'll come down." Howard calls, becoming irritated. "Go and get yourself something in the fridge." Howard turns and runs the few steps to the bedroom. Inside he pulls on his sweater and jeans without bothering to dry off. "What are you doing here?" he calls down to Olson. "My lawyer said that I have to stay away from you or else I'll get arrested." Howard scans his bedroom madly for any object suitable for bludgeoning.

"I have to press charges for you to be arrested. I just want to talk to you. Every day when you follow me I want to turn around and talk to you." Howard can only find an old tennis racquet in the closet, which he clutches and practises swinging menacingly in the air. "Howard? Howard, I wanted to talk to you about the money you borrowed from me when you and Helen got married. I wanted to tell you that you don't have to pay me back." Howard swings the racquet harder and then pulling open his bedroom door he stalks down the hallway toward Olson.

At the top of the stairs he can see him for the first time. Olson is looking out through the bevelled glass of the long, narrow window beside the front door. His hands are shoved deep into his pockets. He is unaware of Howard's approach. The ruddy bald circle at the back of his head has widened over the last few years, it makes a perfect target.

"Howard," he says distractedly as if he is speaking to some Howard he knew ten years ago and now addresses only out of nostalgia, quietly and to himself. "Howard, I was so sick. You don't know."

"It's all right, Olson," Howard whispers anxiously. "I forgive you." Howard raises the racquet up over his head and brings it down with all his might on the top of Olson's head. The racquet knocks Olson to the floor and bounces back into Howard's face, smashing his nose against his cheek and causing him to lose his balance and slide down the remaining three stairs, landing hard on his tailbone at the bottom.

The front door swings open. Helen stands there fumbling madly with a paper bag trying to organize the loading of a gun. Olson is getting up, clutching his head, dazed.

"Shoot him!" Howard screams, "For God's sake, shoot him before he starts talking again!" Helen wrestles the chamber of the gun open with wildly trembling hands, thrusts a fist into the paper bag too eagerly and punctures the bottom, the bullets spill out and roll pell-mell around the floor. Howard scrambles to grab a handful and pushes them at her.

"Here, you only need a couple. Shoot him."

"You do it!" she says, suddenly angry, tears making her

eyes glow. "You're the one who knows how to." He grabs the bullets and the gun from her. Olson is standing now, very still, staring at them.

"Damn it, these are the wrong bullets! These won't even fit!" Howard shrieks and in a fit of frustration begins to throw the bullets at his brother. Olson barely raises his hands to block them. Howard throws the gun and it strikes Olson on the forehead. Olson rubs his temple.

"Helen," he says, "Helen, I swear I killed her before I started beating her."

"Shut up!" Helen screams, throwing herself at him and punching his chest, his arms, his face. Howard watches them for a minute, then he too rushes in to begin beating his brother.

The force of Howard's first blow sends Olson to the floor, his skull cracking loudly on the pale floral tile. And then these two bodies remember each other and they are wrestling on the tiles, rolling, one over the other, punching and shaking and grabbing each other's hair and beating each other's heads against the unconcerned hardness of the floors and walls.

As their desperate energy wanes the punches move more slowly through the air, only rarely realizing a target. Soon they are gasping and panting on the floor, side by side, two men returning painfully to their fifties. Olson gasps deeply, holding his chest with his hand and leaning his head backwards. His voice when he speaks is strained and windy.

"I strangled her with the cord in the hood of her snow-suit. She didn't even have time to be afraid. One minute I was drinking my wine and stroking her hair and saying goodbye and the next minute she was hanging from the cords, from my hands, and when I let her go she fell so loose and fast that I thought it was a trick, it wasn't her, and I started kicking and yelling and beating her. But I swear, she was already dead, I don't know how."

Helen is standing in front of them with the large kitchen knife.

"Olson," she says so quietly that Howard and Olson both

shake their heads and lean forward to listen closer. "I don't know if I can stick this knife in you while you are looking at me so do you think that you could please turn around?"

"Helen?" he says, as if it is incomprehensible to him that she is still on the subject of killing him.

Out of nowhere Howard has a memory, a tiny glimpse of himself standing beside his brother for a school assembly, them both singing the national anthem and everyone standing around them. And he remembers his parents in the ninth row looking down on them and not smiling or singing, just looking vacantly down. He imagines them thinking, 'Yes, those are our sons,' in the kind of meaningless affirmative way that they used to demonstrate that they loved them, if only because they couldn't think of any other way to describe it.

When Howard looks up Helen is hanging on to the knife with both hands. Olson is standing and the knife is stuck in his shoulder. Howard finds himself staring vacantly as his brother lurches, trying to push his wife and her weapon out of his body. There is a blackness eating up the blade, eating into Olson's body.

Howard gets up and walks past them to the kitchen, to the refrigerator. He opens the refrigerator and takes out the milk. He is quite sure that Helen will not notice him drinking out of the carton. He walks around the kitchen drinking the milk. The sounds of struggle become increasingly easy for Howard to ignore. He looks at the closed fridge door, the empty white fridge door. He puts the carton of milk on the counter and pulls open a drawer, looking for the cigarettes that Helen hides from herself. There is nothing in the drawer but a brittle, dusty, unopened pack of red and white striped plastic drinking straws. He closes the drawer. He walks back into the hall past his wife and brother to the hall closet.

He pushes several coats aside before he finds what he is looking for. There's no rush. He pulls the lace out of the hood of his gray kangaroo jacket and wraps an end of it around each hand. He tugs a few times to test its strength.

"It's amazing," he hears himself say out loud, the other

two still too busy to hear him. "The things that can kill you, and the things that should kill you but don't." And he walks up behind his brother and smoothly pulls the cord over Olson's head, around his neck, and drags him back.

Olson tries to get his fingers underneath the cord but Howard just crosses them tighter behind his neck. Olson's neck and face are flooding with blood. He gasps and kicks. He punches wildly at Howard behind him. He falls on his knees and Howard tightens the lace. It breaks; Olson is on all fours on the floor retching and clutching his throat. Howard is staring broken and incredulous at the two halves of lace in his hands. Helen disappears into the kitchen.

"I want you dead. Why can't I make you dead?" Howard asks him. Olson does not answer. Helen stalks out of the kitchen with something in her hand. A sandwich? He couldn't recognize it at first because it didn't make sense. Then, "Of course."

"Hold him," she says and Howard rushes to pin Olson's unresisting form to the floor. He kneels on Olson's arms and chest and he pries his mouth open with both hands. He vaguely remembers this feeling of his fingers in Olson's mouth. Helen opens the sandwich and Olson smells the peanut butter but he doesn't move. She pushes the sandwich into his mouth, taking special care to scrape the peanut butter along his teeth. Howard lets him go. They stand above Olson, looking down on him, occasionally meeting his eyes as they flash around the room.

Howard and Helen walk upstairs together and leave Olson on the floor. They know that he does not carry an adrenaline kit with him. They know that his throat will soon swell and push out all his breath. They have both been with him to soothe him in the past. They go to their daughter's bedroom together. The room seems even tinier, emptier than it did when there was a bed and shelves and a dresser in here. Helen stands by the window and Howard stands behind her.

"Why didn't I think of that?" Howard asks her.

"It's the kind of thing a mother thinks of," she says. They

can hear Olson downstairs beginning to vomit and choke. They can hear the bump and scrape of his arms and legs as they flail on the tile.

There are tears running down Helen's swollen, aging cheeks.

"I don't love you anymore," she whispers and Howard nods.

"No. I know. It's all right," he says, reaching forward awkwardly to pat her shoulder. "It's all right."

UNDER HUNGER

Jenny is eleven. Her arms and legs are long and brown and her hair hangs all the way down to the small of her back. She is standing at the train station in the rain waiting for the next train to come in. Even though it is warm summer rain Jenny shivers and scratches one mud-spattered leg with the other. She leans her bike against the fence and walks away from it. She thinks that she might as well wait on the beach.

The slim stretch of rocky shore by the lake has a steep incline and Jenny runs down quickly, almost running into the water but stopping in time. When it rains the huge open mouth of the sewage drain pours water out into the lake. Some of it runs over, restricting the already spare sitting area to a few inches of beach and the bumpy tables of the taller gray boulders that you can jump along if you need to cross the run-off river. Jenny rubs her arms to warm them up, flicking the rain over her shoulders. She runs her hands over her hair and pushes it behind her ears. She reaches into the pocket of her jean shorts and pulls out a damp brown paper package with a couple of sour keys and a lot of loose sugar in it. She climbs up onto the first boulder and sits, her legs dangling down, her feet in their sneakers, close to the rushing water. She pulls out a sour key and puts the round part between her lips absently. The water in front of her is alive with the sharp pricks of rain. The ducks are quiet, bobbing near the shore with their brown wings folded against their backs. Jenny lies back on the rock, cushioning her head with her arm and lets the rain move over her, the tiny erratic touches gradually claiming more and more of the long surface of her skin. She hears the train coming and through the rock beneath her, she feels the thunderous vibration of it entering the station. But for some reason she doesn't get up.

"You shouldn't lie like that down here on your own." She sits up quickly and sees that he has come down to find her. He has her bike with him, the water rolling off of the green chrome soaks through the side of his still mostly dry raincoat.

"Come on. You're not even wearing a jacket. You're going to get your bike stolen if you keep leaving it unlocked."

Jenny feels her cheeks burn and she scrambles to get off the rock slipping as she does and turning her foot slightly as she lands up to her ankles in the cold run-off.

"Are you all right?" he asks her, stepping forward quickly.

"Yes," she mutters, limping the few steps through the water to the shore, letting her hair fall forward to hide her face.

After they are up the hill and across the tracks, walking along the road together, she having reclaimed her bike, walking it beside her, he says, "Jenny, what are you doing, hanging out with an old guy like me?"

"I don't know," she says and shrugs. She is still hiding her face behind her hair but she knows he is watching her. She can never think of anything to say to him.

When they get to his house he opens the garage door and lets it slide all the way up, over their heads. She walks her bike into the dryness and leans it against the concrete wall.

"This is it," he says, standing by the door with his arms poised to pull it down. "If you're leaving, you have to leave now." She just stares at him. He is as wet as she is now, his raincoat sagging around his shoulders, the front of his shirt clinging darkly to him. He shakes his head at her, steps forward and pulls the door closed.

In the house he snaps at her to take her shoes off because she forgets and tracks the rain onto the carpet. She takes them off, and her socks, and leaves them behind for him to pick up. He follows her as she walks deeper into the house. He is always irritable when she first gets here. He keeps clearing his throat and waving his hands around, showing her all the things that she has seen before. Suddenly she is unsure.

"Do you want me to go?" she says. "If you're busy I don't have to stay."

He stops and looks at her strangely. He looks older when his hair is wet and plastered back. He looks more vulnerable.

"No. I don't want you to go."

They stand there looking at each other, she thinking, he looks old, him thinking, she looks like a baby, until she says, "OK, I'll stay then."

He makes them both coffee, grumbling about how she shouldn't be drinking coffee and she sits at the table in a dry pair of his track pants and one of his T-shirts. She has a towel around her shoulders to keep her hair off her back. He brings the mugs to the table and sits down. His clothes didn't get as wet under his coat so he is still wearing them. The darkness around his chest shrinking as he sits across from her in the small kitchen.

"I was practicing all week," she says without looking at him. "I can read almost fifteen pages in an hour now."

He smiles. "That's great. You learn fast. What were you reading?" He feels his heart being squeezed as she looks at him proudly and says, "*Hunger*, by Knut Hamsun." He nods his head. For a second it crosses his mind that she is pathetic somehow, but he pushes the thought away so that he can watch her hands, wrapped around the coffee mug.

Under the warm dry sheets he holds her against him, still in the track pants but no longer the shirt. The blinds are pulled but they can still hear the rain against the windows. The lamp on the side table is on and she is reading to him slowly, painfully, as he curls around her and puts his lips against her soft shoulder.

"You're not listening to me," she says, as he moves his hand around to cup the negligible swell of her breast.

"How old did you say you were again?" he mutters into her shoulder.

"Sixteen," she says. "You always ask me that. Why can't you remember how old I am?"

"I don't know," he growls helplessly. He moves his hand away from her breast and leans up on his elbow to stroke her hair.

"What is this word?" she asks with an edgy evasiveness, pointing to a word on the page of her book. He reaches for the book and looks where she has pointed.

"Tender," he answers grimly, trying not to betray the ignorance of the question. Jenny rolls on her back and looks up at him.

"I can read, you know. I wasn't lying. Just maybe not as fast as fifteen pages." She reaches her hand up and presses the tip of her thumb between his lips. "You read some and then I'll read some, OK?" she says.

"OK," he says. And they sit up together and he begins to read, tipping the page as subtly as possible toward her, hoping that she is following along.

Sitting in a coffee shop with his friend later, the rain begins to bother him. It should have been gone by now. He feels embarrassed, as if what he has done, what he has thought of doing, might be visible on his face. The waitress nudges him again.

"Do you want a refill?" she says loudly.

"Yes," he says, pushing his cup forward. Even through his irritation he takes a minute to mentally measure her hips.

"So I hung up on her," his friend continues, as the waitress pours the coffee. "A few years ago I would have called her over for one more and then just changed my phone number. But now, I've lost my taste for it. They're so stupid. It's like fucking cats."

He laughs at his friend's coarseness and looks at him sitting across the table, staring at the waitress as she walks away. I'm not like him, he thinks. It's not the same.

His friend looks back to him, suddenly serious and says, "You know, I talked to Davey Barnes last week. We finally caught him screwing one of the boys at the rec. centre. I asked him about it. I came on like, I don't care what he does, just want to hear what he has to say. You know what he tells me?" He leans forward over the table and drops his voice to a slow, secretive hiss.

"He tells me, if you want a little boy, get them before they're six or so, because they won't have the vocabulary yet to tell anyone and even if they do, no one will believe them. They'll figure that he saw something scary on television and just mixed up the facts with fiction. Play the angle, you understand, everybody meant well, but it was just an over-reaction. If you want somebody who'll do things to you, then you want an older kid, eleven or twelve, he says, is best. From about seven to ten is risky, he says, because you don't know what you're dealing with. Before that the kids don't know how to explain it, after that they aren't talking to their parents any-way. But whatever you do, don't touch a kid between the age of seven and ten, unless you've already started on them." He sits up again, grabbing at his coffee cup with both hands.

"I let him finish and then I said, 'Davey, you were always a sick fuck, but now you are a sick fuck on tape.' He just stared at me like I was crazy, like I was the one who didn't under-stand what was going on. And then he said to me, 'Martin, you screwed every woman who ever came to you to help her find housing and you think that you are any different from me.' But they're women, right? Grown women. And I would have helped them anyway, most of them I did help with noth-ing in return. It's not the same as raping little boys that you pick up in the video room of the rec. centre. And I don't even do it anymore. I lost my taste for it awhile ago. I got that fuck on tape. He's going to prison."

He finishes and stares down at his coffee. The table is jerk-ing up and down from the nervous action of his knee.

When he gets home he goes upstairs and Jenny is asleep in the bed. He sits on the edge beside her, pushes the covers around her and lifts her to a sitting position to hold her. My God, she sleeps so deeply, he thinks.

She lifts her head and looks at him. "Did you bring me something to eat?" she says.

"How come you're always hungry?" he whispers. She looks at his face, at the worried sad pull of his mouth. She kisses his lips.

"I don't know," she says. She wraps her arms around his shoulders and the covers fall to her waist. He hugs her tightly against him and closes his eyes. "I was reading one of your books," she whispers in his ear.

"Which one?" he asks her. She doesn't say which book, she just presses closer to him, her tiny breasts so painfully clear against his chest. He rubs her back thoughtfully and says, aggravated, "You shouldn't be here. We should meet somewhere else or we should get you another tutor." He moves to look her firmly in the eyes. "A woman," he says. She puts her head down on his shoulder. She feels the fear that she always feels creeping along her back when it is time for him to make her leave. She doesn't tell him, ever, that there is no place to go, although the truth is that he knows. She looks at his hand loosely holding her thigh. She covers it with her own hand and pulls it up to her breast.

"Jenny—" he starts.

"It isn't sex," she says. "I only want you to hold me. I only want to be close to you. I promise. If you don't put anything inside me, then it isn't sex." And he gives in. Because she is so warm and soft, and because she gives him just enough room to forgive himself.

INSIDE
MOLLY NEWTON

The morning swept in quick today. Like a great gold bird winging across the sky and pushing all the black of night ahead of it. The water in the pond is still smooth and glassy; even the frogs are too awed to start their usual jumping about. I love how cool and clean and friendly this part of the day is. When the world is like this I feel I could do anything, walk a hundred miles, sing something in a proper voice, hold my hand still enough to write my name. When there's no one around I have no trouble pretending that I am just the same as everyone. And I feel brave again.

My mother sleeps deep. She sleeps like a big rock were pulling her mind down to the bottom of the ocean. I sit beside her bed after I come in from visiting the pond and look at her sleeping. Her body is all glorious and even. Her hair loose all over the pillow and her face gone soft and white and young again. Sometimes if she were sleeping rough there are red creases on her cheeks and I try to smooth them away with my finger before she wakes up. Sometimes I whisper in her ear some nice things that she could dream about. When she wakes up she stares at me and she lifts her arms up and holds them out for me and while I am being cuddled she says, "Hello, Molly Molly."

Except that today her bedroom door is closed to me. I did notice that, but thought it must be a mistake. Her bedroom door opening under my hand. There is my mother in her bed, under the sheets. There is somebody else as well in my mother's bed. Big, mushroomy lump guy, bad in my mother's bed. Especially today, *especially* today he is bad mushroomy lump guy. Today is my birthday, my special day that I was born on and made my mother happy. Bad mushroom, mouldy, hairy lump guy. I stomp loud on the stairs to make them feel bad but when I listen they do not wake up so I stomp some more and then I just sit down in the middle of the staircase because what else can I do?

I am fifteen years old. I am skinny and weirdly but I have big pretty eyes, green and blue like cracked glass, and my eyes are cameras because they see and remember pictures of everything. My pupils are permanently dilated because of my secret glamour. My hands shake and my feet twist all around each other when I am sitting in a chair but who cares, even a ballerina does not dance all day. One day I am going to walk everywhere all deer-like smooth and fast, the trees just a green blur beside me. No one will able to keep up or call me back. One day I will open my mouth and every sentence will be sweet, clever magic, like honey, like water, all the secret answers to all the secret questions. One day I will paint a painting of my mother sleeping with the sun coming in the window and falling through her so she glows, herself a bright light through her skin. At the bottom of the painting I will sign my name: Molly. I am Molly Newton.

"Molly?"

It is my mother folding her thin robe around herself.

"Molly, can you make us some coffee and toast? I'll put my slippers on and come down to help you." I stand up and slug, slug all the way down to the kitchen. But I am happy because the day is beginning.

In the kitchen I get the coffee and the filters and I turn on the tap to fill the pot with water. The water must run for a bit because when it first comes out of the tap it's rusty. I put the paper filter in the top drawer of the coffee maker and I spoon the coffee carefully. No matter how careful I am I always spill more on the counter than I get in the filter.

I love how dark and feathery soft the ground coffee is. I love how fat and sweet it smells. One day I will be allowed to drink coffee because it won't upset my electrolytes. I know how coffee will taste when I drink it. It will taste like somebody slowly rubbing circles on my back when I am lying in the grass, and lawnmowers rumbling off in the distance. It is a sad thing to think that maybe I will never drink coffee with my mother. I want nothing like I want to sit across from her at the table and talk about things, have things to talk about, and a way to talk about them.

"Heather," I would say to her. Heather is her real name. "Heather, I have been meaning to talk to you about that bad, mushroom guy." And then I would tell her something brilliant and she would forget him and only love me.

I can talk. I can talk all blue and chatty. But they don't know because I don't want them to yet. Because I am trying on my own. I am trying to make words like my thoughts but I hear the huge deep cragginess of my voice and how I can't control it and I get afraid. My voice reminds me of so many things that make me afraid.

"Is the coffee made already? Thanks, Moll. I guess I was too slow coming down. Do you want toast, Molly? It's your birthday, I'll make you anything you want for breakfast."

But I like toast. I like it so I get the bread out of the wood box and I get the cutting board from behind the silver toaster and my mother smiles and I wait for her to get the knife out of the drawer. She slices the soft bread thick and into the toaster with them! I like honey on my toast, honey and fresh butter. So much honey that it drips over the edge of the toast onto my hands when I am eating it and then when I finish the toast I lick my sticky, glazed hands clean.

"Happy birthday, Molly," I hear my mother say.

It was like the time that we went to see the dolphins. The boat was cutting through the water and the cut water was spraying up into my face. The noise was terrible, terrible.

Only the wet air was fine and tasty. And that man said that when he turned off the boat the dolphins would come and I was waiting and waiting and looking in the water for their backs until finally he turned the boat on again and we went back to the hotel. I think it hurts my mother when she can't give me what she wants.

In spurts I am like everybody else and I can walk straight and my thinking is not so hollowed out and running. Then it seems like I am not wounded at all, just very quiet. My mother looks at me and she sighs.

"Molly," she says, "do you know that I love you?"

I do know.

She thinks I don't remember, but I do. I don't remember lots of things right after they happen but I still remember old things. I remember that he hit me with a brick and she came running into the garage screaming. I know what it takes to change a person. It takes one hit on the side of your head and one hit on the top of your head and one hit on your neck. I am still Molly Newton. I will always be Molly Newton even if Molly Newton is not the same. My father far away.

She would be angry if I could speak because the first thing I would say is, "Where is he?" I do miss him. I don't know why. Maybe only because for a long time he was here and now he isn't.

That guy comes in and sits with my mother and me. He doesn't really talk to me most of the time he just looks somewhere else and asks himself questions and then answers them. Like he were talking to me and then pretending to be me talking back. Like: "Well, Molly, you like the water. I guess one day you'll be a sailor or something." And then: "Yes, I like the water, I will be a sailor."

But today he looks at me and he looks a little sad and he talks to me and his voice is sweeter than I remember it.

"Molly, I'm going to take you on a day trip to Lake Huron for your birthday. We're going to pack some lunch and the camera and then we'll drive there." My mother is watching me, I don't know why.

They pack some sandwiches and I go and sit in the car. It's hot in the car but I like it. I feel all closed and sleepy. The glass window is facing the garage which that guy painted green last summer for my mother. I was upset by the smell of the paint. It was like when my dad was here.

They come out the door with a bag and a blanket and he gets into the car. But my mother does not get into the car. She stands on his side and talks to him through the window he rolled down. Then she looks at me.

"Molly, honey, why don't you move up to the front seat?" she says.

Then we are driving. She stayed behind. I am sitting in the front seat looking at the road. The road is hot and wavy and soon my eyes and ears are hot and wavy and the whole world ripples through me as I am pushed along. It's a long way to Lake Huron but it's always a long way to anything good.

I fell asleep. Now I am awake and looking at his arm straight out moving the steering wheel, and his feet on the black pedal. His arm is wide and brown. It has a hollow just below the muscle and fine, blond hairs that stand up near his wrist. In the hot car I can smell him more. I can smell the detergent left in his shirt and the sweat making the shampoo smell come again.

"Are you awake?" he whispers to himself, still looking straight ahead. "Quiet, little Molly Molly."

I sit up straighter in my seat. My back peels off the seat. Outside, the road looks wet and black in the sun. I look quickly at the sun and then away. It leaves a hot, white finger-print on my eyes.

It was like the time we were driving to Cape Cod and the salmon sandwiches were making the car stink. And my mother was asleep in the front seat and my father was driving and singing with me. Singing *O Canada* in English and then in French. My dad had black hair and a black toenail and the back of his neck was always burned. My dad had a scar cutting his eyebrow in half from playing with his brother when he was little, playing, 'Dodge the Rock'.

It was like the time he broke a chair against the wall and ran out. My mother stood looking out of the screen door crying and I was scared. I crept up to look out the screen door to see what was making her cry but there was nothing but the empty road. The empty road kept her there a long time and then she went up to her bed and lay down and cried some more. It was like a big rock were pulling her mind down to the bottom of the ocean and the ocean were getting all green and hungry. I crawled into bed beside her and she held and kissed my face.

I feel my leg beginning to shake and I lean on it with my hands to hold it still but the shaking is too powerful. I hate this feeling.

"Are you OK?" he asks me. "Should I pull over? Yes, you're probably OK. We'll wait a minute and see if it goes away." He is talking to himself again. But it doesn't go away, it gets worse and now my leg is bumping around and the nerves feel all spidery like there is pain somewhere where I can't see it yet. He slows the car down and pulls it over to the side of the road. He gets out and closes his door and walks around to my side. He opens my door and leans over me to undo my belt and puts his hands on my hips and pulls me around so that my legs are hanging out the car door. I am still holding my leg. I am so unhappy that my throat hurts.

"Let go of your leg, Molly," he says softly, not looking at me just at the leg part of me. I don't want to let go of my leg. He doesn't know what to do. My leg is going to die. My leg is going to break off. My mother knows what I should do. Why doesn't she be coming now, under the car I might slip or anything, my leg, he is too bad. I am going under the place again, the pain place.

"Shh, Molly, it's all right. It's just a small seizure. I'm going to stretch your leg out and hold it and you try to relax. It will stop sooner if you relax. Molly Molly, it's OK."

He is holding my leg in his hands. His hands are big and no shaking. I am all over shaking but less. I lie back on the seat. My eyes all wispy, wet and hot. He holds my leg straight out and slowly makes it calmer. The inside part of the roof of the car has a tear in it. Under the brown felt I can see yellow foam sticking out.

It was like a car we used to have.

I am supposed to be fifteen. I am supposed to be fifteen and not so dumb. Dumb arms and legs that don't listen. Cut them off. I will cut them off, and go to sleep. I hate this way that everything is. He is tucking me back in. He moves all soft and careful. He talks to himself.

"Can you stand on it now? Let's walk around a little."

No. I will not walk around. I do not have to walk all around, stupid.

"Come on, Molly," he says and starts to drag me out. I lean all my weight on him and he picks me up over his shoulder. The shape of my heart is stinging me.

It was like when I was small and sleeping early on the couch.

So we walk a little but almost right away my leg is getting weak and I am still shaking a little so we cannot finish going to Lake Huron. He turns the car around and we are going home, to be safe. He is all nice and quiet.

"Molly," he says, after a long time driving, "your mother and I want to get married." He must think I do not hear him because then he says it again, "Molly, your mother and I are going to get married." And after a pausing, "Molly, you are getting better, you really are."

And then he gives up talking to me and just does the driving because he thinks I do not hear. I hear. But my leg hurts, and my back is stuck on the seat, and I just want to go home. I just want to be home again. I just want to be home.

THE HEART
IS ITS
OWN REASON

"Men are a kind of blade. Even though you can see how sharp and quick they are against another woman's skin it still surprises you when you embrace them and they cut, cut through you, escaping out of your opened back."

"Lana, hush. After all, Gary's dead, you stabbed him in his sleep. Surely it's time to stop picking at him."

Lana is out on bail, staying with Karen until the house is sold. It could be awhile. Not a lot of people want to sleep in a master bedroom where the former master bled slowly to death while the mistress played records that he requested.

"You're telling me that he didn't want an ambulance and he didn't want the police; he just wanted you to play Miles Davis for him before he died."

It made sense that the detective would be suspicious, even sarcastic, but he never met Gary and if he knew Lana, details like this wouldn't even cause him to blink. Karen is looking out of her kitchen window. She is watching her son on the street. He is flying a kite in the high autumn winds. The kite is red and his shirt is red and they tug at each other. The detective came by again last night after Lana was asleep in the guest room.

"None of what she said surprises you? You never heard him yelling for help? What about the music, that didn't surprise you?"

"It surprised me that it was Miles Davis. Gary had a mean temper, but he was otherwise very easygoing, very accommodating."

The detective looked up from his pad and pen, from his untouched tea and the magazine stack that he pushed aside when he took possession of the kitchen table. He looked up at the ceiling and he said, "Is that her groaning up there?"

Davis is nine years old. His kite is red and his shirt is red and they tug at each other. Karen wonders briefly if what Lana did to Gary could be hurting Davis.

'What will he think of us? What will he think of women?'

She knows that there is a threshold in most people's lives before which, at least as far as they know, nothing really bad has ever happened. Let Davis not be there yet. Or maybe let him be there. Let him wet his feet on the death of someone else's father. Maybe that's what was wrong with Lana, no perspective.

Karen wants Davis to stay outside, away from her tired confusion. Karen wants her husband to come home. Karen wants Gary to come and get Lana and laugh and laugh.

The TV is on loud. Davis is sitting too close. He is cross-legged on the carpet, practically smudging the screen with his nose. He needs a haircut. He isn't blond anymore.

After sliding the heavy casserole dish into the oven and setting the timer, Karen goes up to see if Lana needs anything. There seem to be more stairs than there were before.

The guest bedroom door is open. Lana is asleep on top of the covers. The old crib is pulled up beside the bed. Karen creeps up and peeks in. Then she looks over and sees that Lana is holding the baby in her arms. She is curled around the baby and the baby is curled around himself. This room isn't usually so warm.

"Is it time for supper?" Lana asks.

Lana's eyes are wide open in the dark. It gets dark faster every day now, especially in the bedrooms. Karen sits carefully by Lana's feet. She reaches up to touch the baby's back. His little fists are clenched. His eyes are puffy and his forehead is puckered. Lana sits up and drags him up with her. She places him in the groove of her raised legs while she unbuttons her shirt. Karen can see where the milk has wet through the cotton, breast pockets. Lana holds her baby's head while he finds her nipple and begins to suckle. It is such a calm noise that he makes.

There is some light still coming through the open drapes. The window isn't big but it has a friendly squareness. Karen and Lana watch each other. Karen can feel the ghost of Davis's mouth, who knows what Lana can feel.

"Do you think that he dreams?" Karen asks.

Lana shrugs gently and then nods her head. She keeps one hand under the swell of her breast, lifting it to the round and faithful vowel of his mouth.

"What do you think that he dreams about?"

Lana closes her eyes and answers, "He dreams that he is a dog, or a bottle, or a breast. He doesn't know what he is yet."

Karen leans toward her friend. She wants so badly to say something that Lana will understand.

"You know, I don't think it is a sexual instinct. Your baby doesn't take your milk because he wants your breast. Your baby doesn't want to be your lover. It's the other way around. It's the movements that lovers go through that are enactment, just an exchange of symbolic comforts. It surprises you when a man drops to his knees and kneels there in front of you, gnawing at the buttons on your shirt, wanting to get to your breast. And you don't know why he would make himself so much smaller than you or why he seems so greedy. It catches you unguarded. But it is safe. It's only that he is instinctively returning to your body for nourishment."

"Do they all kneel?" Lana's voice is so smooth it makes Karen feel foolish. Why is she babbling about breasts?

"I want to know why you killed him. I know it's between you, and I shouldn't ask, but I want to know."

Lana's eyes are big and dark and shining. In the strange light cast through the window, her body is a collection of half moons. Her shoulder, now shrugged completely out of her blouse, her jaw, the underside of her breast, her hip and her knee are luminous, autonomous bodies in the constellation surrounding the gravity of her length and depth. Her voice is only barely hers as she tells: "I just loved him so much I couldn't stand it. After the baby was born I thought everything was so perfect that I just wanted it to stop right now and stay the same. I didn't want anything to change. I couldn't stand the idea that tomorrow we might fight, or that in ten years we might get divorced, or that one of us might be dragged away by illness. I couldn't stand it. You don't know how it tore at me when he went to work and all day I would think, what if he had an accident, what if he didn't come home, what if he left us here? I would get so sick with it that all I could do was lay the baby down beside me on the bed and grip the brass bars of the headboard and try to think hard enough so that he could hear me: Come home. Come home now."

Davis is playing video games downstairs. It sounds as if he is winning. The shepherd's pie is beginning to simmer, Karen can smell it. The tap in the bathroom is dripping against the cracked porcelain sink. The baby is full, Lana's milk dribbling over his lumpy chin.

"There was a time in my life when nothing really bad had ever happened."

It is possible that Karen is asking a question.

The front door slams and Karen hears Davis drop his joystick and run to greet his dad. She backs away from Lana and runs down the stairs to the door. Her husband is taking his coat off. Her son is hanging on his arm.

"Come upstairs," she says to him urgently, disentangling Davis and pushing his briefcase out of his hand. "Come upstairs."

She drags him by the arm and then skims around behind him to push him up faster. They both see Lana still sitting up in the dark guest room as they pass. They get to their own room and quickly are inside and Karen locks the door behind them.

"What is it? Are you afraid of Lana? Did something happen today?"

Karen tugs off his tie and his shirt and his pants and his socks and his underwear.

"Shut up," she says. Her face is hot as she pushes him down on the bed and forces him onto his stomach. "Shut up."

It takes only a second to slip out of her dress and her panties. She lets her clothes crumble behind her. She lowers herself carefully over his back. For once he is the template. Her legs on top of his legs, her stomach filling the curve of his back, her face in his hair, on his neck. They lie there and he is afraid to move. He is afraid of her hot body.

"I want you to be quiet," she says. "I want you to lie completely still."

TWO
EMPTY CHAIRS

Hattie McDermott was twenty minutes late for our first appointment. She arrived in tears. She introduced herself as Ivy Keller and sat down in my chair behind the desk.

"I know it must be hard for you to look at me," she moans, swivelling the chair around so that she can stare out my window at the lake. "It's hard for me to look at myself. Inside of this fat old body, there used to be someone small and clever but I don't know how long ago she left."

Hattie is seventy-one. She might have syphilis, I don't know.

The pigeons nesting just outside my window throb away and Hattie leans her face against the leather back of the chair. Just for a second I think, Oh no, her tears are going to make the leather streak.

"Why don't we start again. Ivy, what brought you here?"

She looks at me for almost a full minute and I am the one who looks away first.

"I saw a doctor at Centenary Hospital last week who tested me and I knew it, I was right. I'm sick from the life, you know, it took forever to catch me, but now I'm caught, no chewing my leg out of this trap." She is kicking her legs nervously as she watches my face.

"Ivy, do you think we could back up a little bit more. You went to Centenary Hospital." She is nodding her head slowly as I speak. "What symptoms made you go to the hospital?"

"A lot of symptoms," she says, "but chiefly euphoria, and a sudden increase in my sexual libido." She nods her head seriously and smacks the palm of her white hand on my desk. I can't help smiling.

"How old are you, Ivy?"

"I'm seventy-one. Seventy-two in the spring."

"And what did the doctors tell you about your symptoms?"

She swivels away toward the window and then, after a pause, she swivels back toward me.

"Syphilis. But I already knew that. I know all the symptoms of all the diseases that you can get from sexual contact. Every prostitute does." She watches me. "It's all right, you don't have to say anything. I'm the one who's here to talk."

I am in bed but I can't sleep. My husband had a tooth pulled this afternoon, a floating tooth at the back which had been gutted by infection. He showed me the hideous, black, smelly thing, all full of guts, and then he put it under his pillow. It's the codeine, codeine tends to infantalize him. So now I can't sleep because that tooth is in my bed. And I am thinking, and giggling quietly in the soft dark of our bedroom while I think about Ivy Keller, seventy-one-year-old ex-prostitute, stricken with syphilis. The phone rings. I reach quickly to pick up the receiver before it can ring again, my heart speeds up.

"Hello?" I whisper.

"It's me, Ivy," she hisses, "I looked up your phone number. I won't be coming to see you again. My real name is Hattie McDermott and I can't begin to tell you what I think of people in your profession."

She hangs up, and I lie there holding the receiver to my ear.

"She was twenty minutes late for our first appointment. She was crying when she came in and before I could move from greeting her at the door she had pushed past me and collapsed in my chair behind the desk. Syphilis, she said. Can you believe it?"

My colleague swishes the golden remains of his glass of wine in one hand and waves his other hand in the air.

"Do you remember what name she gave you?" I ask him and we strike harmony, saying together, "Ivy Keller."

My thoughts are spinning in circles around a German name.

"Do you think she could be a Munchausen case?" I ask him.

He leans in close to my face with a rheumy, romantic stare before he begins, "Do you know what I think? I think that they all lie to us. Or maybe they all lie a little bit just to see if we can tell, testing, and then they skirt around, sometimes telling the truth or something that sounds close enough so that they can get help if they want it, but not enough so that we can really see them. Do you really think that anybody wants you to really see them?"

I brush his hand away as he touches my hair. I think to myself that he is old and then I realize that he is the same age I am.

"What else do you remember from her visit?" I ask him. Maybe she lied to him because he deserved to be lied to. Maybe she told me the truth.

He shrugs, "I asked her a lot of questions about how she got started as a prostitute, how old she was, what her relationship with her father was like, what her sister thought about her living that kind of life."

"I started because it was offered to me and maybe I was mad or drunk and I started before I could think about it and then it seemed like something that you couldn't go back from. I remember thinking about the first man, that he was old. He couldn't have been more than twenty-eight or so, but at sixteen that was old.

—I told my father I was still in school. When it started to become unfeasible I tried to think of something else, but he died of a stroke before I had to come up with anything.

—My sister hated me, I think, but she didn't tell him, even though she knew. It must have been hard not to. I remember him

raving about me in front of her. I remember her looking at me across the table at Christmas when he was going on about me improving my chances, and her, just a secretary, just a typist. He was wildly supportive of me having a career. Women like you will one day be working for women like your sister, that's what he told her. I thought that was a pretty good joke between us.

—No, I never had a real relationship. I never fell in love with any of my Johns. Honestly, I thought that sex with someone more than once was a waste of time. I didn't even want regulars, much less a boyfriend.

—I quit a couple of times. Once, I tried being a waitress. You're less likely to get beaten up in a back room as a waitress. But your body hurts more. I went home every night, iced my wrists, took a fistful of aspirin and prayed to stop breathing in the night."

"Did you ever imagine yourself married, with a normal life?"

"No. Did you ever imagine yourself as a prostitute?"

"Yes. I guess I have."

"Well, that's the difference between us. You have more imagination."

I can barely track my feet as I rush away from the core of the party to try and find a telephone. I am going to call the hospital and find out if an Ivy Keller was tested for syphilis. Then I am going to call the police and find out if there is any criminal record of a prostitute by either name operating out of Toronto in the mid 1960s to the early 1980s. Then I am going to try and look her up in the phone book.

"Ivy, you were crying earlier, but now you just seem angry. What are you thinking about?"

"I'm thinking about how my mother used to get up at six o'clock in the morning even though she didn't have a job, just to get me out of bed and choose my clothes for me, and make me one pancake for breakfast."

"And that makes you feel angry?"

"That makes me very angry."

A woman by the name of Ivy Keller checked herself into Centenary Hospital on April 1 pretending to be a quadriplegic patient afraid that she might have suffered an infection on her left leg. Her dramatic presentation did not fool the medical staff for any length of time but she was wheeled into a diagnostic space and asked several questions about her injury. As the doctor prepared to confront her and tell her that she was not going to receive a prescription of penicillin, she leapt out of the wheelchair that she had arrived in, crying, "You're all idiots! You're all idiots!" And ran out of the hospital. She was approximately seventy and very small in stature, and although somewhat heavy, unusually sprightly for someone her age, in spite of having sat in the receiving area, contorted in a wheelchair for over an hour before seeing the doctor. She claimed to be American and was going to pay in cash, so no health card or other identification was seen. An hour later an elderly woman tried to fill a prescription for a massive amount of penicillin at the hospital pharmacy. The prescription was handwritten on non-letterhead paper and was refused.

The police have no criminal record of an Ivy Keller but Hattie McDermott placed eight calls to them in April, claiming everything from there being a burglar hiding upstairs when she came home, to being trapped inside as the house burned around her. Hattie never answered the door when the police and the fire departments came. After one of her calls the police broke down her door and entered only to find her asleep in bed. She apparently screamed profanities at them when they woke her.

"A lot of women who become prostitutes have a background of sexual abuse."

"Is that so?" she smiles at me. "The only thing I can think of that would qualify as sexual abuse in my past would be walking in on my grandfather masturbating with one of my dresses when I was around six or seven. That couldn't count though, because I didn't figure out what it was he was doing until after I was already in the life. Oh, I remember it like it was in a movie, me pushing

that big white door aside and seeing him standing beside my little bed, staring out the window with his eyes glazed, rubbing that ugly blue dress against his crotch. It was my Sunday dress."

"Are you religious, Ivy?"

"Everybody my age is religious, aren't they?"

"I got the dates wrong."

My husband leans toward me over the breakfast table. "What dates did you get wrong? What are you talking about."

"Hattie. I asked the police to check for records between 1965 and 1988. But Hattie wasn't sixteen in 1965, I was. Hattie would have been in her early forties already." I push my chair away from the table and begin to stand. "I should have asked them to check between 1940 and 1965."

The morning light is pouring into our kitchen and he is looking up at me.

"You keep breaking my heart," he says.

"What?" I am suddenly disoriented.

"Every time I look at you, you break my heart. I see you sitting across from me at the breakfast table with your hair wet and your robe falling open, and you stare off while your cereal turns to mush and I think, my God, I never would have guessed that someone like you would be the one to kill me."

I lower my head and close my eyes. "I know what you're doing. You're trying to pull my attention back in your direction. I've been very distracted and you are jealous of the amount of energy that I put into my patients. It's very natural for you to feel that something is being stolen from you. I don't want you to feel guilty about it. You are, after all, my family."

"Hattie is not your patient," he says softly and goes back to spooning his cereal.

"My grandfather died of a stroke in his sleep. He was seventy-one. That seemed so unconscionably old then. My father made all the arrangements. I suppose that there really was no one else to do so. He was so formal and self-possessed that it seemed to me as if the

whole process of dying was something that he understood. It was raining on the day of the funeral and as we stepped out of the car to walk through the cemetery for the burial, my father held the umbrella so carefully over my sister and I that only our shoes got wet. They lowered the casket and my father sang some brief traditional hymn and the rain beat over our heads against the black umbrellas. And my father drove home with my mother beside him and it was only after we were herded into the house that he stopped by the door and leaned against the door frame as if he had suddenly taken ill. And my mother put her cool hand on my cheek and held me against her."

A woman named Harriet McDermott has choked to death swallowing razor blades after being refused treatment at Centenary Hospital. She came into the emergency at seven o'clock this morning. She claimed to have been attacked by a dog. She had many small lacerations on her left forearm, none consistent with dog bites. She held her arm and began screaming for penicillin. The doctor on call was the same doctor who was on call the night she came in feigning quadriplegia. He took one look at her and ordered a nurse to clean her cuts with alcohol, bandage them and let her go. Under no circumstances was she to be prescribed anything.

Again she demanded penicillin and began to curse the doctor and the hospital.

I spoke to him. He told me that he just stood there and didn't say a thing, just watched her reddening and screaming and starting to cry. And then she turned and stormed out of the examination area and down the hall into the women's washroom. She had a small box of flat razor blades in her purse.

When she came stumbling out of the washroom, blood was bubbling out of her mouth. She was choking hard, a terrible windy sound following each breath.

We can only assume that she was trying to manipulate the hospital into treating her.

"Hattie? Hattie?"
"I'm sorry, I was somewhere else for a second."

Her house is a small brownstone only a few blocks away from mine. The landlord gave me a key because I told him that I was her doctor.

There are heavy dark curtains pulled closed over every window. When I pull them open I see that the red felt wallpaper is badly faded by the light. There are no pictures anywhere, only the rippling surface of an antique mirror at the end of the hallway by the front door. Hattie has twin beds in her bedroom, pressed up against opposing walls. Only one bed is made up. A thin, striped mattress lies naked upon the frame of the unmade bed. In the bathroom wineglasses filled with dry, brown, scentless potpourri line the narrow counter. I turn the taps on and off. I splash water against the side of the sink. I open the medicine cabinet. There are vials and vials of penicillin: pills and liquid, spoons, and syringes, and under the counter as well, and later I find on the shelf of the bedroom closet—enough penicillin to—enough for sure.

There is a criminal record of prostitution for Ivy Keller and one for Hattie McDermott. They are sisters in the life. Married name, Keller for Ivy McDermott. Ivy McDermott /Keller died at sixty-five in her home on January 1, 1989. Cause of death: cerebral hemorrhaging. Likely related to the sudden manifestation of a latent case of syphilis.

"Do all old people have blue eyes?" I realize suddenly that I have said this out loud.

"A lot of old people have cataracts," she says coldly, turning her face away.

"I'm sorry, that was very rude of me."

"It's all right. It must be hard to control yourself all the time listening to your patients. Ask me anything you want. I like answering questions, especially personal questions."

I am staring deeper and deeper into the crevices around her eyes and mouth. There seems to be no end to them. "Ivy, what colour was your hair?"

She laughs, a fluctuating weak laugh. "I don't remember. It was a light brown when I started dyeing it, but I was so young that I don't know what colour it ended up. By the time I wanted to grow it back it was so gray streaked I couldn't stand it. Let's see. In the forties it was a sort of golden brown, smooth and waved. In the fifties it was a dark brown, black if I left it in too long, and tied up most of the time. It was red for two years at the end of the fifties and then I found the most marvellous natural, pale blonde, and I wore it any way that anyone liked as long as it could stay that colour. That was my favourite colour.

"*My sister never dyed her hair, she had beautiful copper-coloured hair and she could type eighty words a minute, even before she had ever used an electrical typewriter. We had an apartment together once before she got married. When we moved in, the land-lord asked us if we had any cats. Yes, I said. What kind of cats? he said. A tabby and a small black cat, I said. Oh, but no lions or tigers or ocelots or anything. No, I said, they're not big game cats. Because we had a lion here before, he said. It walked on a collar but it scratched all of the mouldings on all of the doors to pieces. Sure enough, there were huge gouges running along all of the doorway mouldings. I suppose that they could have been made by a dog. Who am I to tell if that landlord was blind or a liar?*"

A KIND OF
APOLOGY

Sam asked me to write everything down. He said that I never have to send a letter or show anyone but that I should write it down and really look at what I've said afterwards. I don't want to fight anymore so I will try to do as he asks.

It was eleven o'clock and I was driving us home along the highway. Sam was asleep in the seat beside me, Ian was asleep in his baby chair in the back. We were coming home from a day visiting my parents' house up north. We stayed too long after dinner. I don't like driving in the dark; I'm not a good driver, even when the sun is up and the weather is good. Sam's head was rolled over on his chest and he was starting to drool. I shouldn't have said that. He gets embarrassed when I tell people that he drools in his sleep. I like it, though; it's funny the things that seem sweet when they're done by someone you love. When you have a new baby, even their shit is sweet.

Ian had been so good that night. He ate all of his dinner and didn't cry at all. Mum held him and bounced him and he laughed and stared at her as if she were the funniest, most beautiful woman in the world, which she is, of course.

I get hypnotized by the road sometimes. It's the long, smooth journey and the landscape collapsing in around you as the night falls. The soft momentum of the acceleration and the buffeting of air against the windows when they are open just a crack. I drifted into the other lane just for second but it was such a tight corner. The headlights of the other car burned my eyes so that I didn't see the crash, I only felt it.

I remember opening my eyes and feeling pain in my legs. I looked at Sam and he was awake, staring around with his face covered in blood. "Oh my God, Sam," I said, "why isn't the baby crying?" Sam twisted around to look in the back seat and then he looked at me, but he didn't say anything, and I lost consciousness.

I don't know if you can hear things when you are in a coma. I don't think so. I didn't hear anything. When I struggled up for a second here and there the pain was almost like a noise, but I didn't see Sam hanging over me, or the doctors trying to help me, or my mother and father. I know you must have wanted me to see you. I'm sorry. It was only my eyelids that were open.

I've been home from the hospital for months now but it still seems like only a day.

Ian would have been two yesterday. I bought him a brown felt cowboy hat with a bead to hold the string under his chin. I've been sitting in his room all day with the hat. Sam asked me to come out but I pretended not to hear him. He won't come in here anymore. I wanted to call you and ask if I could give the hat to your son but Sam says that you don't ever want to see me again. I can't understand that; I don't think it's fair. I do understand why you called the police, and I am sorry. I'm so sorry. If I could just explain to you. My son, I know that your son isn't Ian, but if you would just listen to me I could explain to you how he sort of is Ian. Why can't you understand that I need my son and that my son is still there?

I had four miscarriages before we finally carried all the way. When Ian was born I was depressed even though we had wanted him so badly. I was exhausted, my arms and legs felt hollow and weak, my stomach felt horribly collapsed, my breasts were full, itching and aching, and my head throbbed all the time. I didn't feel like I could hold him or nurse him, or even look at him. Sam did everything the first three months. And he had to take care of me too. I couldn't get out of bed. Every day Sam brought me meals on a tray and coaxed me to eat. He dragged me out of bed by the arm and pushed me into the shower. He called my mother for me and brought the phone into the room to try and persuade me to talk. I couldn't do it. I couldn't do anything.

One day Sam carried the baby in and sat beside me on the edge of the bed and murmured to him and to me in the same voice. Then he put him down beside me. I think he was trying to get us used to each other, like I was the jealous old pet and he was the wriggling new kitten. Sam told me that we had to name him; how did we let three months pass without naming him? Sam asked me what I wanted to call him. He said, "Maybe if you'd just start calling him something you would feel different." I asked him if he had been calling the baby anything; I knew that he had. Sam said that he been calling him Derek. I didn't like the name Derek; I said that I would rather call him Ian, after my father.

Ian had rheumy blue eyes for the first week but they seemed to get darker every day. They were almost black by the time he was killed.

When I woke up in the hospital after the accident I was in a room with someone else. The hospital was extremely over-crowded so people were being rushed out of intensive care, where everyone has to be kept in a room alone, to a sort of midway between intensive care and a regular stay room, where two patients could be closely monitored as they shared a space usually set aside for patients who can afford to pay for privacy. The woman in the room with me was old. No one came to visit her except the doctors. She had had several heart attacks in one week and I could hear her breathing laboriously through the thin floral curtain drawn between us. When Sam and the doctor came to explain to me that Ian was dead and that they had donated some of his organs to save other children I remember turning my head away and staring at that curtain. I heard the old woman start to cry.

Please understand, at first I hated Sam for letting them have parts of our son. I felt like Ian had just been chopped up and no one cared that he was going to be a little boy and they had turned him into a grocery store. I told Sam that he should have waited, that he should never have made that decision without me. I screamed at him. I said that he didn't love Ian, that I'm the only one who lost a child. I screamed at him every time he came to the hospital and I cried all through the night after he left. They gave me my own room free of charge because they were afraid I was going to give the old woman another heart attack.

But even when I was screaming at Sam I could feel it, I couldn't face it, but I could feel the squeeze of guilt in my chest, because Sam wasn't driving. I was driving. Sam and Ian were both asleep.

It was so strange leaving the hospital without Ian. I had cried and cried for days on end but at some point I just couldn't cry anymore, so I stopped, but nothing had changed. I left the hospital without yelling and without a single tear. Sam had already bought a new car and that twisted inside me.

The first month was the worst month of my life. I didn't sleep and neither did Sam. We didn't talk to each other. There was nothing that either of us wanted to do for the other. We went to a psychologist together and then apart, but I never said a word in his office. Whenever he asked me a question I just shrugged or sighed. After a month had passed I told my family doctor that my arms ached so badly, all the time. He looked at me sympathetically and said, "Yes. Parents often find that their arms ache for years after the death of a child."

And then your letter came. It was like an injection of light into my brain. I don't know how it could not have occurred to me that somewhere out there someone was alive because of Ian; and so maybe, someone was keeping Ian alive inside of him. I read your letter over and over again. I read it in my head and I read it out loud. I was disappointed that it was only his kidneys inside your son and not his eyes or a piece of his brain. I know how sick that sounds, I'm sorry.

But you sounded so happy and I could feel his presence radiating from the paper in my hands. For the first time I felt better. I cleaned the house from top-to-bottom in three hours that day. When I showed Sam the letter he sat down in a chair and read it over and over again and then he started crying. I looked at him with his face buried in his hands and his back seizing with every sob. It was the first time since the accident that I was able to feel sorry for him.

We almost had sex that night. We lay in the bed together anyway, holding and kissing each other. We had lain in that bed oblivious to each other for so long.

So, you see, at first I was really happy for you. You were my sign of Ian's goodness. This miraculous thing he had done, and I'm sure that I was starting to come to terms with his death. You were so nice to send us that picture. I stared at it, wincing at the scars on his little tummy. I couldn't believe that here was a living little boy that my little boy had saved. A little baby saving another person's life. Surely he should have been rewarded for that.

I don't know when I started looking at that picture and thinking that Ian was in there, inside your son's tender, scarred, little tummy. When you invited us to visit I was so nervous I had diarrhea all week. Sam was in good spirits, walking around, talking about Ian. We talked so much together that week. We talked about every single thing that we remembered about him. Sam talked about his little head, the round skull, the flat part at the back. I talked about how Sam had told me that Ian had rubbed all his hair off tossing and turning in his crib when we first brought him home. I remembered Sam sitting beside me on the bed, lifting my hand and putting it on Ian's stomach. I started to feel his wrinkled, bony fingers under my hand. I started to think that I could smell him. Everywhere I turned he was in the corner of my eye. There were a lot of times just after the accident when I thought I could hear him crying, but now I heard him gurgling and burping and blowing bubbles. I had everything but the weight of him lying on my chest, or in my arms. I can't tell you.

I think you must realize that I was, and still am, on a lot of painkillers because of what the accident did to my spine and my legs. I'm not sure if I healed so fast afterwards because I just forgot that I was hurt too, or maybe I thought that I didn't deserve to be sick or to be cared for. So it could be that I was not thinking straight when we were at your house, although I still must tell you that I feel you overreacted. In the car on the way over, I said something stupid about going to get Ian. Sam looked at me when I said it. I know he was worried.

My first thought when you came to the door was how pretty you are. And so young. You and your husband have time that we don't have. That's all right. I don't even want to have sex anymore. I don't want to have another baby. I just want my baby back. But that's all right, I'm not as bad as you think.

You came to the door and your husband came up behind you with your son in his arms and your son looked at us and started laughing like we were as funny as a pair of monkeys standing on the porch. We all started laughing. You took us in and took our coats and I looked in the closet when you were hanging them up and I saw your son's little coat and his boots on the floor. We all went into the livingroom. I could smell the fresh coffee when we walked in. We all sat down and your husband put your son (Why can't I remember his name?) down on the floor to play between us and you told us all about the operation and how scared you were, but I wasn't really listening. I was looking at your son. I can't explain how I felt staring at him. I was seeing every tiny detail of a living little boy, his elasticized corduroy pants, the sauce on the front of his shirt, the way his dark eyelashes curled. He was playing with these giant pieces of toddler Lego on the floor between us and I remember thinking, Maybe he'll be an architect.

It started to really irritate me that you were still talking. I know that's a terrible thing for a guest to say. When I looked up and noticed at one point that you were crying, I have to say that I didn't care. I looked at you and thought what a bitch you were, crying, when you have a baby in front of the people who don't have one anymore. I looked around your house and I thought it was ugly. Much richer than our house, but tacky, over-furnished and messy. Sam tried to hold my hand but I pulled away. Your husband had his arm around you. Sam took out a package of pictures of Ian that he brought to show you. I was shocked by how few there were. Not big, glossy, studio pictures of a well-lit baby, propped up in front of a forest painted on a screen, like you have on all the shelves. Just a few Polaroids of him in the bath and some Kodaks of Sam feeding him, or him lying beside me on the bed. I watched you look at the pictures and I know, for a second, that I saw something on your face, that you were thinking your son was prettier than Ian.

And then you smiled at me, like my partner or confidante, and you said, "Why don't you spend some time with Ian while we show Sam the rest of the house?" Of course you didn't say Ian, you said your son's name, but I heard wrong. You all went off and I slipped onto the floor and picked up some Lego. I don't know how to play with Lego but I tried to copy what your son was doing and just stick a piece onto another piece. I held out my hand and took his little hand. He smiled at me and I pulled him onto my lap and felt him leaning away from me to try and grab another piece of Lego. I don't know what possessed me to whisper in his tiny warm velvet ear, "Ian, Ian," but your son twisted his face up to look at me and he leaned against me, lifted his shirt and pointed to his scar and I was lost.

Without even saying a word I picked him up and we were in the car before I knew it. He started crying because I was moving so fast and carrying him a little roughly. He was crying hard in the car, harder after I started it and harder still when we drove away. He kept taking off the seat belt, it was way too big for him and he could just slip out of it, so it was hard to drive because I had to keep reaching over to buckle it and to slap his hand. He was screeching by then. His face was so red. The blue veins in his forehead stood out. I tried to calm him down but I couldn't. I pleaded with Ian to calm him.

Don't you ever even try to understand that I would never have hurt him? That I would have brought him back. I just wanted to say good-bye to my son. I had him screaming beside me and I reached over to put my hand over his mouth. I was sure I could hear sirens. I ran off the road and then back onto it, I was speeding, and then the car hit a pothole and we stopped. I stopped us. I put my head down on the steering wheel and I listened to my heart pounding and I wiped away blood on my lip from biting it when we hit the pothole. Your son was still crying. I didn't know where to take him. I didn't know where we could go or what I was doing; I was scared of what you were thinking. I was scared of myself. I thought that you would find us right away. I got out of the car and I pulled him out with me. I started walking as fast as I could. I took him to a park. I didn't think that there would be anybody at the park in the fall. And I sat on the swings with him in my arms. I held him so tightly that he stopped crying. He was scared. I had no right to scare him. By the time the police found us we were both shivering with cold. You took him back and you looked at me so hatefully. Sam didn't look at me or speak to me at all.

And now it's all over. I can't believe it's all over. I was going to bring him back. I was scared too. I know I can't explain to you. I know you can't forgive me. I know how I sound and that you can't trust me. But I can't tell you how much I miss

him and how sometimes I just want to die. Please forgive me.
I'm so sorry. I'm so sorry.

STEALING KAY

Anna is eight. Her sister, Kay, is only four. They are in their backyard on the swings. Anna pumps her legs and swings so high that the chains holding the wooden board under her jerk as she falls down again and then pumps her way back up. There are a lot of birds sitting on the telephone wires in the field which starts where the lawn ends. Kay is not swinging. She is sitting very still. Her feet dangle loosely, far away from the ground.

"Kay, I can see Wales from here. I can see Nanny and Grandy! Kay, you have to move your legs, like this. Look, look!"

Anna has seen bigger kids jump off the swings when they are up high. At the park they jump off and fly through the air and land in the sand. Their feet make deep marks where they land. Anna is not allowed to jump because she could crack her head open. Still, she thinks about it, she wants to, but she is scared to. She wonders if her head would open right up or if there would just be a huge crack running across her face and around the back of her skull, under her hair. Anna looks at Kay. Kay is slumped against one of the chains. Kay is slipping off the swing, onto the ground. Anna digs her feet in quickly on the way down and falls forward. Kay is lying on the ground. Kay is not moving.

"Mum! Kay fell off the swings!"

Her mother turns slowly away from the kitchen sink as Anna bursts in in a panic.

"You mean you pushed her off."

"No! No, this time she fell. She was just sitting there and then she fell."

Her mother looks out of the kitchen window to where Kay is still lying. They start running together but Anna's mother leaves her far behind. The screen door slaps the door frame several times before the latch catches.

They are all in the car. Their father is driving too fast. Anna can feel how fast they are going. Their mother is sitting beside him. They do not talk. Kay is curled up in the back seat with her head on Anna's lap where Anna has pulled it to be. Kay is hot and sweating. Anna touches Kay's bare arms and legs. Kay's whole body is wet.

The elevator moves so fast it makes her dizzy. Kay has already gone to one of the rooms. There is someone on a stretcher jammed in beside Anna. A nurse is trying to keep the stretcher from hitting Anna's shoulder. It doesn't work. The person on the stretcher moans quietly. The person is so old that Anna cannot tell if it is a man or a woman. The nurse is supposed to take her to her mother and father.

It isn't fair that she can't see Kay yet. She is the one who told them about what happened. One of the doctors takes her into a closet. He turns the lights off and shines a flashlight on her forehead. The doctor is much bigger than her. Her face is level with a mysterious brown smear by his waist.

Cerebral meningitis. Cerebral meningitis is what is wrong with Kay. Anna is all right. The couches are brown leather. There are Oreos in the vending machine. You cannot see her, she is in intensive care. You cannot go in there. They shouldn't have let her know where she was if they didn't want her to sneak.

Intensive care is a room full of machines. It is very small and dark in intensive care. The bed is lifted high by steel bars that cross each other. Kay is hard to see, she is so much smaller than the machines. There are tubes stuck in her arms. Anna can see that there is room under the bed for her. She sneaks in quietly and climbs through the bars and crouches underneath her sister. She whispers her sister's name but there is no answer so she keeps whispering it. It is a comforting name to repeat.

"Kay, Kay, Kay, Kay—"

They found her but they aren't mad. They are still not talking. She is sandwiched between her parents on the couch in the waiting room. At some point she falls asleep.

Her father must have carried her to the car because she does not remember coming home. She is in her bed and her father has come in to wake her up. He sits on the edge of her bed and looks at her hand resting in the middle of his own. He is still dressed in his suit. He smells like the hospital. He smells like his smell is hiding something. He says that Kay is a little better and they will go back to the hospital after breakfast, and then he stands up and walks stiffly out of her room. He does not kiss her good morning. As Anna pushes off the covers she sees that she is also dressed. Her shoes are on the floor beside her bed. She is happy that they are going back to get Kay. She looks at the French dolls on the print of her wallpaper as she squirms out her clothes. One of the dolls looks like Kay, blonde and blue-eyed, and one of them looks like Anna, dark hair and green eyes. These dolls are probably sisters too, she decides.

Downstairs, her father has sliced up bananas for breakfast. He has changed out of his suit and washed his face but his hair is still sticking up in back. When Anna points this out he smiles and licks his hand to smooth it down. He gives her a glass of milk. He does not know that she has juice for breakfast. She doesn't complain. She eats the slippery pieces of banana and tries to listen to him as he talks on the phone. The cord is stretched around the corner of the wall so that he can stand in the next room and talk. Anna wonders where her mother is. Her father finishes his call and smiles at her as he walks back in and hangs the receiver back on the wall. There are bananas and pears on the print of the kitchen wallpaper.

"All right, I'm going to take a quick shower and then we can go. We should bring one of Kay's nightgowns for her and maybe a toy. Why don't you go and choose those for me while I'm getting ready?"

Dads are silly, why would Kay want her nightgown in the daytime? thinks Anna.

There are more days after this but she is not sure what order they go in. They keep moving Kay to different rooms.

On one of the days Anna goes to the old room by accident and sees the empty bed. Her mother stands beside the bed, talking to the janitor who is mopping up broken glass and a dark, thick, red puddle. Anna stands in the doorway looking at the puddle, looking at the bed that Kay is not in. Her mother turns and catches her eye. She rushes to Anna. She grabs her by the shoulders and shakes her.

"It's Ribena," she says. "I dropped a bottle of Ribena."

There is a girl on this floor who is Anna's age but Anna does not want to play with her because she is bald and her skin is grey. There is a baby that she sees a nurse holding.

"What's wrong with the baby?" she asks.

"He has a hole in his heart," the nurse answers. "We're going to put a patch over it."

"Like with jeans?" Anna stares at the baby and wants to ask to see the hole.

Her father goes to work and comes to the hospital afterwards but her mother stays there. Anna gets dropped off in the morning and goes home with her father at night. She still does not get to see Kay, except from the doorway when her mother comes to greet her. Kay just lies in bed. She still has tubes in her arm. She has styrofoam cups taped around her hands to keep her from pulling them out.

Lots of people talk to Anna when she is playing in the waiting-room. One of the doctors comes up to her when she is drawing a mouse for Kay.

"Are you Anna?" he asks.

"Yes," she answers, concentrating harder on her drawing.

"Well, Anna, did you know that your name is a palindrome? Do you know what a palindrome is?" he says, crouching beside her.

"Yes, it's a rhinoceros," she answers, sticking her tongue out as she draws a horn onto her mouse's nose.

"No. That's a pachyderm. A palindrome is when a word is the same backwards as forwards, like, sit on a potato pan Otis."

"What?" Anna is irritated because so many people think they are so smart.

"Here, I'll show you," and he takes the pen out of her hand and draws on her paper, right in the middle of the mouse that she was going to give to Kay.

Sit on a potato pan Otis.
sitonapotatopanotis

"See?" he smiles and hands the pen back to her as he puts a hand on her back.

"That's stupid," she tells him. "Who would want to say something stupid like that?" She snatches her paper away, crumples it up and throws it in the garbage as she stomps out of the room and away from him.

In the hallway she opens a door and slips inside in case he tries to follow her. She is in the linen closet. There are doctors' coats and hats and pants folded up on the shelves. She decides to play dress up.

She pulls down one of the gowns and searches for the arm holes. When she gets her arms in she has to pull the sleeves up so that she can get into the pants. The pants are harder to get into and she falls over as she pulls them on. She stays on the floor because she has pulled a whole shelf of clothing onto herself. From the surrounding pile she finds a hat and tries to tie it around the top of her head. The door opens. There are four people dressed like she is, staring at her. Anna is swimming in green cotton.

For the first time she is in trouble. She is relieved to be yelled at. Not only did she break into the linen closet but she tried to lie to them, telling them that she was a patient, that she had leukemia. Someone has gone to fetch her mother. Someone new has come to yell at her.

"There is nothing funny about leukemia," the doctor says. "This is a hospital, not a playground. Don't you think your parents have enough to worry about with your sister being so sick? They don't need you tearing around, making trouble."

With your sister being so sick. Anna's hands and cheeks go cold.

"Is she really sick?" Her voice is tiny. She begins to tremble. The doctor sees this and calms down.

"She is sick, or she wouldn't be here. Kay has had a brain hemorrhage and she is having an operation right now. It would be better for everyone if you stayed quiet."

Her mother has arrived. The doctor puts an intimate hand on her arm and draws her away from Anna. They talk in low adult.

"What's a transfusion?" Anna asks quietly.

Her mother looks at her and answers, "It's when they give someone, someone else's blood."

"Whose blood is Kay getting?" Everyone shifts their feet uncomfortably.

"I don't know, sweetie," her mother answers.

"How do you even know it's from a person, then? They could give Kay dog blood!" Anna is shouting. "You can give her my blood! I'll take the transfusion. You can't just put blood from someone she doesn't even know in her."

"You're too young to give blood, Anna. Calm down." Her mother and the doctor are grouping together, moving toward her.

"You can't just do anything you want to her!"

The doctor turns to her mother and tells her quietly, "We could use Anna's blood. Kay's blood type is rare and you can't give blood because of your thyroid condition. It's not very much that we need. It might make her quiet." Anna's mother is irritable. She waves her hands as if to shoo away the situation and says, "Fine. Fine. Give her Anna's blood. Do whatever, just do something."

"Well, come on then, Anna. We'll take your blood now."

"Go with him, Anna. He's going to take you for your needle."

The doctor takes her by the elbow and leads her away while she thinks about the word, *needle.*

She has to lie down on a bed. She has to let them tie a rubber thing too tight around her arm. She munches seriously on a cookie and stares at the wide needle sliding into her arm. When the needle is in the nurse pulls the rubber band off of her arm. Bright, red liquid comes rushing out into the tube and runs toward a plastic bag sitting in a metal device. She watches the bag rocking back and forth. She watches it grow as it fills with the red liquid.

"That's my blood?" Anna asks.

When they have taken her blood to Kay, who is still being operated on, Anna goes back to the waiting-room. She wants to save the mouse drawing that she threw in the garbage but when she looks in the bin it has already been emptied. There is a window in the waiting-room. It looks out over the highway. From behind Anna comes a little girl's voice.

"I know what they're doing to your sister."

Anna doesn't turn around. She knows it is the bald girl. She squints her eyes as she looks at the highway. She wants to turn the zipping bodies of the cars from beetles into a snake.

"Do you know how they figure out how much blood to give a person in a transfusion?"

Anna still does not turn.

"When they're operating, they mop up the blood that comes out with sponges. Then they put the sponges on a scale and weigh how much blood they soaked up."

Anna turns her head and looks into the bald girl's gray face to see if it is true. The girl nods seriously. "I've had lots of transfusions," she says.

The next day, when Kay is told about the blood, she starts to scream. Anna goes and stands in the doorway so that Kay can see her. Anna has to show Kay that they didn't kill her to get it. Kay looks from where she lies, metres away in the bed. She waves. Anna waves back.

"Honey-pie, do you play the guitar?" This woman plays the guitar. She doesn't look like a nurse. The guitar is big and black with a silver line around its edges. This woman plays and sings in the waiting area. She plays *Where Have All The Flowers Gone*, and the kids are supposed to sing along to the chorus:

Where have all the flowers gone, long time passing? Where have all the flowers gone, long time ago? Gone to young girls every one, long time ago.

Anna sits at the woman's feet. She has to sit in front so that the woman can keep an eye on her. She can see the woman's fat, white knee lifting and falling under the orange print skirt. The bald girl is sitting beside Anna, trying to hold her hand as she chants along with the song. Anna is singing too, trying to be good.

The song is finished and the woman is tuning her guitar. The strings are a little green and they twang sharply as she strikes them and twists the metal knobs at the top of the guitar's neck.

"Have any of you boys and girls ever seen an angel?" she asks pleasantly. "I saw an angel once when I was driving home in a rainstorm." She pauses and looks them over. "It was a dark and stormy night, and I couldn't see a thing for the rain on my windshield. I was on a deserted highway and I was starting to fall asleep at the wheel. I would drift away and the car would swerve and then I would wake up.

"Well, the last time that I did this, when I opened my eyes there was someone standing on the road in front of me! I stepped on the brakes hard and they squealed and I swerved like crazy. I went right through that person's body. I saw his face as he passed through the front of the car and through me and out the back. He was a young man, all white and frightened and trying to say something.

"When the car did stop, not a second later, I jumped out and stood in the pouring rain and the dark just looking around for him. But there wasn't anybody anywhere. When I went to get back in the car I saw that I had been driving off the road and my car had stopped not three feet away from the edge of steep cliff. If I hadn't braked for that man I would have driven straight off into the ocean!"

She nods her head firmly as she finishes her tale and assesses her impact on the children. They are all huge-eyed and silent, staring at her. She looks at Anna and smiles.

"I saw your sister today, honey. She's doing much better. Such a pretty little thing, your sister. All those blonde curls, she's a regular little angel."

Anna is huge with her anger. She jumps to her feet and smacks the woman in the stomach.

Turning around she tumbles and kicks over the other children as she struggles to get to the door.

She runs down the hall toward her sister's room. At the door she sees that her mother is not there. Kay is the only one in the room. She sits up when she sees Anna and Anna runs in.

"I'm taking you away," Anna tells her and Kay watches as Anna drags a free stretcher from the other side of the room over to Kay's bed.

"Ow!" Kay says, as Anna pulls the IV roughly out of her arm and rolls her onto the stretcher.

"We're going to escape," Anna tells her and starts to push the stretcher out of the room. Just as they cross the threshold into the hallway, their mother comes out of the bathroom and sees them. Anna starts to run. The stretcher moves fast on its wheels, pulling her along with its momentum. Kay is lying on her stomach, looking behind them, watching the gathering crowd chase them.

"Where are we going?" she screams.

Anna jumps onto the back of the speeding stretcher.

"We're going to Cape Cod!" she screams back.

She jumps off just in time to whirl the stretcher into the open elevator. Her mother is calling her name, yelling for her to come back. They are only steps away. Anna presses the button and the doors close. The dizzying elevator whips them down to the ground floor. As the doors open, a shocked troupe of medical staff and patients witness Anna shove her sister on the stretcher out into the lobby. She runs and catches Kay and the stretcher heading for the automatic front doors and the parking lot. For a second she is afraid that the doors will be locked and she and Kay will smash into the glass, but they slide obediently apart just in time.

As they head out into the brilliant sunlight Anna screams to the world, "She's my sister! She's mine. She's mine!"

And Kay raises her hands up in their cups and chimes, "I'm hers! I'm hers!"

TO BE
A GOOD BROTHER

It was something to have a sister like Iris. An older sister, all long and white-skinned with hair that fell in coils all over her pointy, freckled shoulders. Simon was nine or ten and she didn't like him, never had, but she left the bathroom door open all the same. It was spiteful and vain of her brushing out her hair while she stared at herself in the foggy mirror and the water rolled down her bare, articulated back. Simon leaned against the doorway, looking and not looking and then looking again.

She must have left them behind on purpose; he can see that now. Could she really have gathered up her robe and towel and brush and makeup and pushed past him so crossly and left something so mind-bogglingly significant as her underpants behind? No. Underpants; for a ten-year-old boy a mountain of sexual evidence.

Simon remembers how carefully he shut the door, sure that she would come running back for them at any second. How he leaned against that door and stared at them, all rumpled and damp on the furry pink bath mat beside the smooth, soft-shining tub. Iris: giant, mean, cold-voiced, womanly Iris, with her very long legs and her catty, smooth, secretive crossing of them beneath the kitchen table at dinners, on the couch beside him watching television. Iris: the only available example of actual moving breasts on an actual moving girl. He was sure she knew all of her favourite shirts became transparent when the sun shone behind her. But just in case she didn't know Simon kept quiet, deathly quiet, and very still.

Without even bothering to urinate Simon grabbed the underpants up and running like a quarterback he streaked wildly out of the bathroom with one arm braced ahead of him to knock aside the invisible armies of shocked relatives. He ran down the stairs, out the door, through the backyard, and into the field.

As he ran the long dry grass whipped against his legs and he could feel himself gradually weakening. Up ahead he strained for a signal, a flash of light beckoning off of the metal of an abandoned car at the edge of the field. He chugged desperately forward and then stopped, suddenly, and stood. Deep in this field he could not even see his house behind him. There was nothing to hear except for the slight echoes of distant birds and a sluggish whispery rustling. The afternoon sun shone steady and hot on his face and chest. His legs, scratched and brown in his shorts, trembled under him. His heart beat hard and clear against his ribs. He let his body ripple down toward the ground, to lie in the rough, sharp, dry grass. He wiped his sweating forehead with the underpants and something in his brain was set alight by the mysterious sweet smell of them. Some new part of Simon stood up.

He held the underpants to his nose and breathed again, shy and shallow breaths growing slowly bolder. He remembered something he had heard and he stuck out his tongue very slightly to check.

"I'm a very bad brother," he said out loud, opening his eyes to look through the eyelet at the edge of the underpants at the clear even blue of the summer sky. "I'm very bad, very bad."

And then a miracle happened. As his hand drifted vaguely, indecisively over the strange contents of one of his short pockets, some kind of seizure, some kind of shivering, soft, seizure rolled through him and out through his desire and evaporated except for a silly, silky spurting. And he was relieved. A good brother again. A brother who would chastely dig a hole in the ground with his own hands to bury his ungrateful sister's underpants to protect her honour from strangers.

So you can see, can't you, how it's all Iris's fault?

Simon slammed the door when he came in and stomped angrily up toward his room. His mother, standing by the oven in the kitchen, called after him, "Simon, do you want some cookies? I just made them."

"No," he yelled back, louder than he needed to. It may not be the biggest punishment, he thought to himself, but it's all I can bear.

He rushed to his room, pushed the dresser against the door, threw himself on his bed and tried to figure out what had happened and how he might have changed. He did not want to see his mother. His head started to pound just imagining his mother looking into his eyes, a sickened look freezing across her face when she saw what her little boy had done. I'll never do it again, he thought as firmly as he could. I will never do it again. I will almost never hardly very much do it again.

He met his wife, June, at the library when he was twenty-five (all that mad tugging and humiliating blistering long behind him, he thought). The library was a small stone church which had been gutted, carpeted and filled with books. June was standing near one of the windows reading a book. Because she was short-sighted and too vain to wear glasses, she held the book so that it almost touched her nose and scanned the lines with madly crossing eyes.

"What are you looking at, fatso?" was the first thing she said to Simon. It made his heart gurgle with love.

June was almost a foot taller than Simon. She snapped at him frequently to stand up straight, sit up straight, stretch out. "Don't you know women want to feel a little overwhelmed? Squeeze my hand harder," she said. "You're just a big lump of mashed potatoes shaped like a man."

He used to drive her to the landfill at night and they would stare at the brilliant blue torches burning off the methane on the dark slope. "It's so beautiful," June whispered. "It smells bad, but it's so beautiful."

Simon took this as his cue to fumble over her and they struggled awkwardly in the small car for a few minutes until Simon gasped and June's eyes drifted closed.

He hadn't seen Iris since she left home for college so there was no reason to expect her to show up for the wedding. But she did. Just as June and he were standing in front of the minister, about to begin, Iris swept in, storming down the aisle and up behind him to smack him in the back of the head.

"You should have told me," she said.

"What?"

"You didn't invite your own sister to your wedding. I'm Iris," she said, turning to June and shaking her hand politely. "Go on. I'm here now," she told the minister and went to sit with his parents. Simon didn't hear a thing from then until June nudged him.

"I do. Say, I do," June urged.

"I do. I do all the time," Simon said.

Behind him, his mother started to cry.

"It really would have been better to let her stay with my parents," Simon whispered to June in their bed on their wedding night.

"She's your sister. I really like her. It's only for a few days," June answered reasonably. "Aren't we going to make love?"

"Fine. Fine," he grumbled turning on his side toward her. June reached down to find him stiff and ready. "It's been like that all day," he told her softly, touching her face, watching her smile. In another room he heard the discreet padding of his sister walking around, finding something to do until a rea-sonable amount of sleepiness could overtake her.

She'll lie in the bed, he thinks to himself, guiltily urging his honeymoon along. She'll lie in the bed between the sheets and the sheets will fall around her body. They'll cover her cool legs and nestle against that soft triangle and the tips of her.

Simon stares at June below him. Her eyes are working behind her closed lids, her face looks strained. You're so far away, he thinks. You're so far away.

"She's been here two weeks!" he yells as the door closes behind Iris.

"What's the big deal? You get along, she's nice. Let her stay. You don't want her to get stuck choosing some lousy, expensive apartment, do you?"

Simon rolls his eyes. "You don't understand," he says. "She leaves things around." June stares at him as he sputters and grapples with something. Simon begins to bang his fists on the table like a toddler banging on the tray of his high chair. "She has to go," he urges. "She has to go!"

"Simon. Don't be a baby. She's staying and if I hear one more word about it I'm going to push my fist down your throat, grab you by the foot and pull you inside out, do you understand?" Simon smiles weakly and nods his head. "Good. Now be a good little thing and do the laundry for me."

Simon nods his head again and then smiles until his wife walks out of the room.

They're not that much alike. In the musty basement Simon is sorting the bundle of clothes into wash loads. Actually, Simon looks more like Iris than June does. They are about the same height now, June is bigger than both of them. Iris has cut her curly red hair so that it spills around her face like a teenage boy's, June has long red hair, frizzy, but only properly curly when it's wet. June and Iris have very similar personalities, though. They are both unrelentingly mean to Simon. They both pinch, kick or smack him every time they pass by close enough. Simon picks up a pair of June's underwear. He stretches them out and holds them up to look at them. They are pink lycra, shiny as the inside of a shell and wearing thin across the back. He tries to be a good husband by picturing his wife standing in her underwear in front of him. When this image fails to arouse him he adds a large white feather boa to the image and tries to picture his wife dancing for him like a stripper. Never having actually seen a stripper he has trouble picturing her movements, imagining that she would just wiggle her shoulders to make her breasts swing back and forth and kick with one foot and then the other. Maybe she would blow kisses at him and wink. Not working. No good.

"What kind of thirty-year-old man has never seen a stripper?" he says out loud, suddenly disgusted with himself.

"Never seen a stripper, never slept with a prostitute, never hidden a dirty magazine in the back of the toilet in a plastic bag. By God, I've got a lot to do today!" he exclaims. When he looks down at his hand he sees that he has dropped his wife's panties onto the dusty cement floor and he has begun carefully fingering the small, white eyelet cotton briefs that he was so sure to have buried twenty years ago. "Oh no," he squeaks. He scoops the laundry up in his arms, holds it against his chest while he lifts the lid of the washer, pushes it all in together, slams the lid down, and turns the machine on. "Take that," he says and he runs upstairs.

He walks down the street with his hands shoved deep in his pockets and his shoulders shrugged up to his ears. When he reaches the corner store he pauses for half a step and then he pushes the door open with his shoulder and walks in. The magazine rack is enormous. His cheeks are throbbing with embarrassment. He has to stand on his toes to see what he is looking for. How you choose is beyond him. The clerk looks up from behind the counter, shakes his head, and looks down again. He is reading the *TV Guide*. Simon sees a woman standing on the other side of the food rack beside him and he tries to cover his face. He waits until she pays and brushes past him out the door before he walks up to the clerk. The clerk is approximately the same age as him, Indian or Greek, with a short haircut, wearing a neat plaid shirt and a red wool tie. The ordinariness of his appearance soothes Simon.

"Listen," Simon begins, "what kind of pornography do you sell the most of?" he asks the clerk.

"Are you a film student?" the clerk asks dryly.

"No."

"Women masturbating, or else women having oral sex with other women. Far left of the shelf. We do have some specialty magazines under the counter if you think you might be interested in retarded girls or pregnant women."

"I don't think that will be necessary," Simon says as he turns on his heel and rushes out of the store.

In the shop down the street he buys a package of cigarettes and some gum. He walks to the park and sits on a bench.

"I'm weak," he tells himself. "I'm a weak degenerate." He coughs on the cigarette until tears roll down his cheeks.

In the dark sticky theatre there are other men and a terrible briny smell. They all try to sit as far apart as possible which is difficult because the theatre is small and almost full. None of them take their jackets off. The film has just begun. Simon has only one eye open and a hand up to his cheek to shield that eye.

The woman on the screen looks a lot like Iris looked when she was sixteen. She trails across the screen toward a man lying like a bird pinned to a bed by a huge arrow. She begins to undress. Simon is trying hard to watch only the part of the screen that she is on. He hums to himself to block out the dialogue. Someone behind him hisses "Shh—"

She has a long, flat stomach. She is in her underwear now. Her ivory-coloured breasts lifted against the white bra panels. A lovely dive under the curve of her belly. White underpants. Not quite right but close enough.

"No more," Simon whispers. "Just stay like that, just a few seconds, I'm almost—"

But then there is the shucking of the remaining clothes and the flailing and the pumping. The gross slick tube of the actor and the slappy wet sounds. Simon covers his mouth and gags. The tension in the theatre is compressing him. The man beside him is beginning to shake, weird rickety breaths moaning out of him. Simon leaps up and runs away.

How many times can one man leap up and run away in one day?

I can't stand myself, he thinks as he rushes around the streets blind with misery. I can see it now. I was seeing my sister every time I touched my wife. I was lying in that field, breathing that smell, suffocating as the cotton was drawn into my nostrils and mouth—I can't make love to anyone but my sister! I'm very bad. Very bad.

On the corner ahead of him a woman is standing, her short skirt hiked up to reveal stockinged legs. She sees Simon walking toward her and she smiles as he gets closer. When he makes a sharp left and enters the laundromat she scowls.

OK. What-is-the-plan? We are in a laundromat but we have no laundry. There are a lot of women in this laundromat and one thing women do not like is a guy with no laundry standing in a laundromat looking at them, Simon thinks.

The woman closest to him looks up. She has short, dark hair, dark eyes and dark skin. Simon smiles at her nervously. She looks away. He steps forward very carefully. She looks at him again. Again he smiles. She looks away. He takes a step forward. She spins to face him. "Listen—" she starts in angrily, but it is too late. Simon has reached forward, grabbed a handful of her soiled underpants shoved them in his pocket and burst out of the laundromat, running and running and not letting up until he gets home.

"Simon. Simon, what are you doing in there? Come out for dinner. Simon. Simon, are you all right?" June hammers on the bathroom door and then pauses to press her ear against it. She falls forward into Simon as the door opens.

"Here I am," he announces boldly and strides past her, tall and confident.

In the kitchen they sit around the table and Simon is the most talkative one in the bunch. "Can someone explain to me—" he goes on and on. Iris watches him.

"Let me ask you something, Iris." Simon says, "Is there any chance, any chance at all, do you think, that you might not be my real sister?"

Iris does not think this is funny.

"That was mean, Simon. Iris didn't say anything to warrant that," June jumps in.

"Forget it, June," says Iris. "He's a funny twisted little gnome who thinks nobody can see what he's doing. Well, let me tell you something, brother, you are transparent as glass. You swelter that out, OK. No, no cookies for me, Mom. My fingers are all dirty and my sister's underpants are gone." Iris's voice is mean and familiar.

"What is she talking about, Simon?" June's voice is just a weird little buzzing beside him. Iris gets up from the table and walks out of the room. June follows her. When she comes back she has Simon's jacket in her hands. She stares at him as she reaches into the pocket and pulls out a pair of underpants and holds them out to him.

"Whose are these?" she says, beginning to cry. "They're not mine. They're not Iris's. Simon, where were you today?"

Simon's stomach is churning and his brain has been squeezed dry. His wife stands before him with a fistful of evidence and the pain is unbearable. "It's not what you think," he moans. He opens and closes his mouth desperately as she stares at him. Finally he finds it: "I'm having an affair," he says, smiling helplessly up at her, opening his arms to the air.

MADDY AND ADAM

Maddy is dreaming. She lies on her stomach with her cheek and nose crushed against the pillow. Her eyelids twitch. Her eyelashes are wet. In her dream she opens her eyes and sees the long panelled hallway outside one of her brother Adam's classrooms. She begins walking down the hall. As she walks she looks through the cut-out windows in the doors. As she passes each room she watches the same scene progress, as if she were watching a film being shown in short spurts.

The professor stands in front of the blackboard. On the blackboard, drawn in chalk, is an illustration of a woman's genitals taken from an anatomy textbook. Beside this detailed first drawing is a clumsy sketch of a chocolate bar, half unwrapped. There is a title over the drawings: Course Requirements for an Honours BA. The professor is gesturing wildly, back and forth, between the drawings and the title with a pool cue. The blue chalk on the end of the cue leaves electric coloured circles wherever it touches.

There is a long row of female students standing single file in front of the professor. Some are tall and fair, some are dark and squat, they are all undressed. Each student in her turn steps up to the professor. With his cue he points either to the genitals or to the chocolate bar. If he points to the genitals she hands him a chocolate bar. If he points to the chocolate bar she drops to her knees and begins giving him head. As each transaction is concluded he strikes the girl across her neck with the cue and then she disappears.

"I'm going to tell!" Maddy calls out helplessly, screeching out of her dream. The green porcelain clock on the wall is ticking. Everything is all right.

Maddy is seventeen. She has been sleeping with her brother's friends for six months now. Adam makes the arrangements, primarily among the same group of his university peers. Adam is studying to become an engineer. He and Maddy live together in a small flat just off-campus. At one time they were both foster children placed in the same foster home.

"Maddy? Are you all right, I heard you yell something." This is the voice of her brother's silhouette in the doorway. "Time to get up now anyway. Peter's going to be here soon." He steps into the room and walks over to the side of the bed. With one hand he pulls the covers off and with the other hand behind her neck, he lifts her gently to a sitting position, slides the now free arm under her knees and picks her up. She slips back into sleep even as he is carrying her, bumping against his chest, toward the bathroom.

The bath is too hot and she has to bite the inside of her cheek to keep from leaping out right after he slides her in.

"Does your hair need cleaning? I can't remember if we washed it yesterday or not." Adam is soaping her back, drawing circles around her shoulder blades and a long line down the middle. Maddy is sitting with her knees drawn up and her arms wrapped around them.

"Yes, my hair is dirty."

He presses the front of her shoulder to persuade her to lie back. She can feel the air touching the parts of her body that leave the water and the heat that rushes across the newly submerged skin. Maddy leans her head backwards and goes completely under the water. She opens her eyes to see the blurry figure of her brother leaning over her.

When she is clean and flushed, her black hair hanging down her back, sleek as a wet seal, she sits on the window sill. She drinks her coffee and looks outside. There are fifteen shiny, black birds on the telephone wire. There are burnt leaves scattered in the street. Adam is on the phone in the other room. The doorbell buzzes and Maddy unfolds herself to respond.

When she opens the door Peter is standing there. He smiles at her companionably and steps in. "Hey, Maddy," he says. "Did you just get up? I can wait if you want to eat breakfast. Is Adam here? Peter catches sight of Adam, who waves at him while holding the telephone receiver against his cheek with his shoulder. Peter strides in to see him and Maddy goes to her room. She doesn't have to dry her hair. Peter likes the smell of her soap and shampoo. He likes to coil her long wet hair around his hands. She should probably brush her teeth.

When Peter and Adam enter her room she is sitting up on the unmade bed, rubbing cocoa butter onto her calves. She looks up at them and puts the jar of butter on the night table. She picks up her towel from where she dropped it on the floor and covers her pillow with it. It is only because of the rules that Adam stays, they know that Peter is all right.

Adam sits in a lounge chair in the corner. He and Peter swap school anecdotes while Peter gets undressed. Maddy stares back and forth at them while they talk. Everything about university fascinates her.

When Peter is undressed, his body long and warm and freckled, he looks at her and she lies back. He reaches down to open her robe and she shivers. As he lays down on top of her she wriggles to get more comfortable beneath him and he puts his big hand quietly around her throat and says, "Maddy, Maddy, hold still."

I have a BA and a Masters degree, and a Ph.D. No, two Ph.D's, one in Engineering and one in English. I am a lawyer on Mondays, a veterinarian on Tuesdays, and a doctor through to the weekend. On the weekend I write my novel.

Peter and Adam leave together, punching each other on the shoulder. They both have a class to get to. Adam takes a twenty-dollar bill out of the battered leather of his wallet and gives it to Maddy before he leaves, so that she won't have to stay in the house today. The other one hundred and eighty dollars goes toward rent, food, tuition for Adam and a tuition fund for Maddy. She will be free all day. Nobody else is coming over until after dinner. Maddy is still standing in the doorway of her bedroom after they leave. She did not bother to put her robe back on. Even though the curtains have been closed she bends over to sneak past the window in her nakedness. She wants to look out the peephole at the hallway.

For some reason every time that Adam leaves she has a sudden seizing fear. She is alone.

"Maddy, Maddy, Maddy, what are we going to do with you?" she whispers to herself while she sits on the subway car, moving toward the museum. Wedged into the seat beside her is a fat blonde woman chomping down smelly Doritos. Maddy opens her purse and takes out her book. She is halfway through *Anna Karenina*. She opens the book to the bookmark and stares at the page. After a few seconds she flips back a few pages and stares again. A man in blue jeans and a blue jean jacket sits down on the other side of her. He takes the book out of her hands and turns it over to see the cover. He looks at her and smiles. "What is a girl like you doing reading a book like this?" he asks.

She blinks. For a second Maddy thinks she recognizes him and her heart speeds up painfully. She doesn't answer, she just stares back into his eyes. He hands the book back and apologizes. She opens it anywhere and pretends that she can read it. She can't even see the words on the page.

Everybody knows, she thinks. They can tell by looking at me.' Maddy looks up and across the aisle into her reflection in the dark pane of glass. She sees the ghost of a pale girl, pretending to be clever.

They sit in silence at the kitchen table. Adam made mashed potatoes to go with dinner. He did it to please Maddy because she likes them. His irritation gathers as he waits for her to say something. She drags her fork through the potatoes, flattening them over everything else on the plate.

"Someone new is coming tonight," he tells her. He notes her slumped posture and her flat, loose hair with disgust. He finds something accusing in her appearance. "You are going to get cleaned up before he gets here, aren't you?"

Her fork goes still and she mutters, "I'm not feeling well. My stomach hurts. Can't you ask him to come another time?" Usually Adam is so good about what she wants. It is one of the rules.

"No." He thrusts his chair out from the table and whisks Maddy's plate from under her raised fork so quickly that some of the mashed potatoes fall onto the carpet. The doorbell buzzes. "Go to your room and get ready." He steps quickly into the kitchen to drop off the plates, and then rushes to the door.

Maddy is in her room. She is not on the bed where they will expect her to be, she is lying beneath it. Her thoughts are getting bigger and faster, throbbing against her skull. This is not right. This is against the rules, she thinks. She is supposed to meet him first. She is supposed to talk with him and tell him the way it will be. She gets to say if it will be or not.

The carpet is bristling against her hot cheek. She can see the light of the door opening. Someone's bare feet walk up to the bed. Adam does not come in.

He dragged me out by my wrist. It hurt. This is not right. This is against all the rules. Where is Adam? He is supposed to be here. I know he can hear me. Maybe he left the apartment. And I don't get to go on the bed. And I don't get to roll over.

I am going to get a scholarship and take my tuition and I won't leave you anything. I'll get a degree in psychiatry and have you committed. I'll become a police officer and arrest you. I'm going to write a book and tell everybody what you did to me. What you all did to me. Adam, Adam!

"Maddy? Maddy? Maddy?" He's here. The room is quiet. Still on the floor, she tries to cross her legs tightly enough to obscure the origins of the pain. Adam kneels beside her. She reaches for his limp hand and brings it to her mouth and bites it and then pulls his palm up to cover her eyes. He leans down over her, covering her curled-up form completely with the arch of his body. She is startled to realize that it is Adam's shuddering travelling through her. She smells his shirt and his skin and his sweat, and she remembers his fourteen-year-old body, afraid as he is now. Once it was Adam who was traded for her.

Moving together, they clamber onto the bed and scratch off what is left of their clothes. Lying, facing each other, connected by their touching foreheads and drawn up knees, their intentions are invisible. They could be praying. They could be waiting to be born.

Adam begins to whisper. Maddy opens her mouth and he whispers against her cheek while she tries to breathe: "Maddy was an angel. One night she fell out of the sky into the dark arms of the forest. A group of deer hunters found her in the morning, asleep under a tree. One of her wings was broken and her legs were scratched from falling through the branches. They watched her sleeping for hours because they were afraid of her and they didn't know what to do. She must have been so tired.

"When one of them finally worked up the nerve to touch her hair it was so soft he cried out. Watching her sleep so deeply made them restless, craving. After a while they decided that there could be no harm in touching her. So they rolled her in the grass and ran their hands through her hair. They stuck the tips of their fingers between her lips. They pressed their rough faces to her belly, to her arms, and then finally, toward her legs. They were foolish enough to think that they could take advantage of an angel. When the first one touched her wrongly she opened up her eyes, her black and wounded eyes, and she looked at them and they all caught fire and died. Did you hear me, Maddy? They all caught fire and died."

It is the middle of the night. They are naked, in a bed, in a small room, in the dark. They are scared. They have no one. They are remorseful for the things that they have done to each other, to themselves. If everything that they have done is terrible, and they know it, then let Adam put his hand upon her breast. If there is nowhere for them to go now, and they know it, then let Maddy slip her hand down to hold him. Let them fall asleep like this.

THE PIGEON

The red, plastic receiver shakes as the phone rings. It is Jonah's brother. Their voices are so similar that to a third party, it would sound as if one person was affecting a conversation with himself.

"So, how about this. A woman on a cruise ship has an unhappy love affair with a soldier who is a little cocked. She breaks off with him and the next day he approaches her while she is sunbathing on the deck. He hands her what at first looks like a large gift-wrapped perfume bottle. He stands there, smiling at her as she pulls off the ribbon and opens the lid. Inside is a hand grenade with the pin pulled out. It must have been defective to last even that long. She screams and without thinking, tosses the hand grenade to a waiter who was coming to ask if she would like to order a drink. The waiter drops the grenade and it rolls down the deck and he chases it. When it hits the railing it explodes and the waiter, who had just come to his senses and turned away from it, is killed. The woman is charged with involuntary manslaughter. The soldier jumped off the boat and nobody knows what happened to him."

Jonah's brother loves to relate these stories.

"You made that one up," says Jonah.

"Yes, but it could happen. It probably has happened; I just haven't found out about it yet."

Jonah snorts doubtfully into the phone and shifts the receiver to his shoulder while he searches his jean pockets for something. He has been searching his empty pockets ever since he turned forty. The doorbell rings.

"Listen, I think that's her," he says and his brother whistles sharply.

"Call me the second you're through," his brother begs. Jonah promises and hangs up. He skips a little as he tries to prevent himself from running to the door.

She is facing away from him when he opens the door. He clears his throat when she does not turn around. He sees that she is dressed casually, almost sloppily, in bleached jeans that hang low on her narrow hips and a thin T-shirt which has been stretched and faded by wear. There is a tiny hole in the shirt at the shoulder and he sees that her skin is brown.

She turns in one step and lifts a pair of sunglasses off of her face to look at him. Her nose is small and freckled. Her eyes, some indiscriminate colour, squint at him.

"If you're Jonah, I'm the sin eater your brother hired," she tells him and he nods and steps aside to let her in. As she steps past him he notices for the first time that what he thought was a large handbag is actually a cardboard pet box.

Once they are inside he is impatient to get to the dining room but she wanders around looking bored as she takes in his house. The cardboard box meows every time it smacks against her hip. Jonah nervously gropes in his pockets. He decides to go to the dining room and begin setting up. He will wait for her there.

In the dining room he flips a plastic sheet onto the table. He pulls off his sweater and undoes his jeans. He holds his stomach in as she walks in through the doorway to watch him finish undressing. He lies down on the table. She walks over to him. She looks him over carefully. Her long, straight hair falls over her face and she pushes it back with her slender hand. She is wearing a ring on her engagement finger. For a second Jonah pictures some enraged, seven-foot-tall, high school quarterback bursting in and hollering over his middle-aged nakedness and himself, on his knees, begging for leniency.

Shaking these images away, he speaks to her.

"OK, the tray is in the kitchen. Bring it in."

She walks back toward the door she came through. A few seconds later she returns with the tray. At the light switch she stops and balances the tray against her stomach while she turns the dial all the way up. He feels the lights rising. He feels them warming his nakedness. He feels the plastic sticking and marking his back and his ass.

She walks over. She puts the tray down beside him and gets on the table herself. She crawls over him and they are face to face. He can see past the collar of her shirt which has fallen forward. He can see her breasts leaning against the confines of the white bra cups.

"Am I supposed to take my clothes off too or do you want me to just start right off?" she asks.

His cock lifts slightly. No, he thinks, that would be counter-productive.

"No. You keep your clothes on. Just take the food off of the tray and start putting it on me."

"OK," she says. Climbing over him, she sits cross-legged beside his head and starts picking at the tray.

She picks up the tomato slices first and lays them carefully over his belly. One, two, three of them, cold from the refrigerator. He shivers and clenches his teeth. Then the cucumber slices around the tomato and sprigs of parsley around the cucumber. Some of the parsley rolls off, tickling his side as it falls.

He feels himself rising again and he tries to divert his attention. He is afraid of scaring her. He looks around the room. He reads off book titles from the shelves. *Tropic of Cancer, Lolita,* no, that doesn't help. He tries to think about the paper he is writing: *The Last American Slaves.*

The last American slaves are children, he repeats his thesis to himself. Well, to be more accurate, the last slaves are children, convicts, and the mentally ill, but not in his paper. He chuckles to himself as he remembers how clever and funny he was when he designed the little checklist in his paper: A slave is an individual whom the law does not recognize as free. A quick test to see if you are a slave is to ask yourself: a) Can you vote? b) Can you sue? c) Can you move?

She is sliding a warm omelette onto his chest. As it settles, it burns.

"Ow, SHIT!" he yells but is afraid to move so he just pants through his teeth as he becomes aware of the thinness of his skin.

"I'm sorry, I didn't think it would be hot anymore." She lifts a corner of it and blows on his chest. The hairs sting as they move.

"It's all right," he says, "It's probably cool now, just lay it down again."

She releases it and it flops back into place, a slightly more comfortable temperature. A little trickle of butter slides into his armpit.

"OK if I cut out for a second and have a cigarette?" she asks him. She is already reaching into her pocket for the pack.

"No. Well, I don't know, I kind of wanted to get on with this."

She glances at him as she flicks her lighter against her jeans, once to open it, back to light it. She dashes the flame across the cigarette, inhaling expertly.

"Well, what are you, like fifty?"

"I'm forty," he groans.

"Still, I think it will take awhile to absorb." And she walks out and leaves him there, the smoke hanging over his face.

After about ten minutes he gets anxious. He sits up to try and see where she is. The omelette slides into his lap, the cucumber and tomato slide between his thighs. He moves back to pick the food up and feels something stab him in the ass. He holds himself up by one arm and pulls a threaded needle out of his behind. It must have been on the table before he laid the sheet down. He must have left it there when he tried to mend his jeans last night.

Disgusted with himself he throws the needle carelessly onto the floor and lies back down. His whole body is slimy with food. He almost hopes that she doesn't come back.

"Hey, have you got any hooch?" she calls brightly as she strides back in. She smells more like she has been sunbathing than smoking.

"Hooch?" he asks.

"Yeah, gin or rum or something."

"In the cabinet," he grumbles and motions with his hand. Hooch, he thinks bitterly. How can young people appropriate such phrases in such a cool fashion and still manage to sound dismissive? What would she think if I had used the word instead of her?

He hears the ice cubes rattling before he sees her. She stands over him with her arms crossed, grinning and throwing a big glass of gin down her long, young throat.

"You're a mess," she says. She reaches over to the sideboard where she left the gin bottle and refills her glass and throws that one down her throat too.

"How old are you?" he asks suddenly. She gives him a sly look. His voice has betrayed the answer he is looking for.

"I'm eighteen," she answers lightly.

Christ, she's lying, he thinks miserably. He lifts his head a little ways so that he can bang it quietly, repeatedly against the table. She thinks this is funny.

"What are you banging your head for? I'm the one who has to suck off an old man."

Does she have to be so coarse? he thinks. He looks at her. Her cheeks are getting flushed from the liquor. Across her neck and chest a tiny rash is spreading. Her eyes look sleepy and she is swaying as she smiles down at him. He feels a guilty pang at the same time as he feels a lustful one. I am ridiculous, he thinks. Look at her, look at how smooth her hands are. Look how awkward she is, standing there with a bottle of gin in one hand and a glass of ice cubes held against her cheek by the other. She is still practicing to be a woman. He closes his eyes and sighs heavily.

"You are not here to suck me off, you are just supposed to eat the food off of me."

"Oh, and that's better?" She falls to a sitting position

beside him and begins picking the food up and putting it back on him. "What happens to me after I eat your sins?" she asks. Her voice has gotten higher, more childish.

"I think the idea is that you gain knowledge." She snorts and begins to laugh convulsively, falling forward, her face pressing into his side. Her breath is warm against his thin skin. She is completely drunk. Almost experimentally he moves his hand against her head. Her hair is soft and unbearably clean. She stops laughing but she stays there by his hip. Her breathing is slower and deeper now. He raises his arm and strokes his hand down her back. He can count her ribs as he passes over them. She is very still. He can not tell if she is frightened. Stroking back up toward her head he feels a quiver run through her once, and then again. Something in him shifts and he pushes her head over his hips toward his erection.

There is a loud gagging noise. It is not coming from her, but from under the table. The girl shrieks and drops off the table. He sits up. He doesn't know what is happening.

"Help me!" she screams. "Tiger swallowed a needle!"

He jumps off the table. She is sitting under it. In her arms a large tabby cat is choking and convulsing, his eyes popping out of his head, his jaw, stretching and stretching.

"He swallowed a needle! I saw it shoot into the back of his throat!"

Oh God, his heart is beating fast. The phone book. He can't even remember where he put it. He doesn't know what to look under. The cat is going to die before anyone gets here anyway. The girl is holding the cat, trying to soothe it. Her voice is a panicky moan as she says: "No, Tiger, no, Tiger, no."

Trying to be decisive he kneels down and takes the cat from her arms. She looks at him, begging him to know what to do. He can barely hold the cat, its body rolling with the convulsions. He tries to pry open its mouth to see if he can reach the needle. As he holds its jaws open it suddenly considers him the new threat and claws at his naked thighs.

"Leave him alone!" she yells and punching Jonah in the jaw she grabs the cat and cradles him against her chest.

"Oh, stop it, stop it," she sobs, her tears falling into the beige fur and being shaken off as the spasms move through it. Then, as if by miracle, the cat gives an extraordinary gasp and hurls the needle out, into the carpet as it exhales. It looks up at the girl, now crying openly, her arms wrapped around her knees, her fists wiping her cheeks, it looks at her and looks at Jonah, then walks mildly to the corner and begins licking its paw.

Jonah stands up. He walks over to the table and picks a towel off the tray. He wipes at his body. He sees how much has gotten on the carpet, onto the velvet seats of the chairs pushed up to the table. He finds his jeans and takes his wallet out of the back pocket. He unfolds the bill that he has waiting for her and he walks to her side. Putting a hand on her shoulder he says: "Come on, get up. I'll call you a taxi."

She looks up at him. Her face is brilliant red and wet. He tries to guess her age but finds he can't. He can't tell how old anyone is anymore.

"Are you sure?" she asks him. He nods. "I don't need a cab," she says, "I live nearby."

She gets the cat into its box in record speed. She takes the money without a blink. At the door she offers to come back some other time but Jonah shakes his head. She skips down the stairs to the street and walks off, holding the cat box up to her face and whispering into it as she goes.

Jonah closes the door as the phone begins to ring. There is a large mirror in the hall and he can see himself. His hair is wild and grey. His body is slick with butter and vegetable juice. He holds his stomach in and finds that he still has a paunch. Moving up to the mirror and leaving the phone to clatter and call for attention, he examines his face. He sees it. Around his eyes and mouth and emerging through the ever widening span of his forehead. The little vixen has left him there, helpless and foolish, with all of his sins drawn up to the surface where everyone can see them.

THINGS YOU TOW

Ida is feeling tired and restless. Nothing good ever came out of this feeling. The apartment is small even when they don't move around. Porter is lying in the narrow cot pressed up against the wall. Ida is dragging ice along the feverish length of his bare arms, over the raised, trembling muscle, into the elbow, toward the blue wrists. He lies there, immobile, and stares at the low bulge of the ceiling.

"I can hear mice scratching inside the wall," he whispers.

"Don't worry. They can't get out," she answers.

The ice melts quickly into her palm, its form dissolving, adopting the shape of her skin, the lines of her hand, before surrendering into the tiny currents of the rivers running over Porter's skin into the sheets.

She scoops more ice out of the clay bowl nestled in the skirted cleft of her lap. She lifts his arms to rub the fresh, cold corners of the cube along his ribs and over the wide wall of his chest. She moves quickly, wanting to cover as much area as possible before it melts. He starts to speak again. She puts the rest of the cube in his mouth and holds his jaw shut.

"Shh, love, you have a fever, try not to think."

He shakes her hand off and coughs down the ice. His eyes open wide staring at her. He opens his mouth. He closes his mouth. He opens it again and whispers tightly, "Ida, I'm going to leave you. Things are going to happen to you and I'm not even going to know."

She puts her cold, empty hand to his cheek, to his forehead. She moves her fingers through his damp, unwashed hair. Through the wall behind him she can hear the old woman next door shuffle to her couch and click on the television. The sudden surge of voices combining in laughter drowns out the faint sound of a dog barking outside.

When at last he falls unwillingly to sleep she stands up and steps to the bureau. In the top drawer she fishes out her cigarettes and takes them with her to the wooden chair by the window. She lights a cigarette and sits, her arms folded and resting on the window frame, her face leaning out into the evening cool. Down the street the dog is still barking, his black mouth pointed to her, gulping. The sound moves with effort toward her, as if it had a long tunnel to roll through before it could reach. As she inhales, the lighted end of the cigarette flares. In front of her she smells trees and sidewalk and a little way off, the water. Behind her is the heat and dust and medicine of Porter. He is very sick. What is she going to do?

She scratches an insect bite behind her ear and shifts her sticky thighs beneath her long cotton skirt. When she finishes the cigarette she will have to sterilize a knife.

As she waits for the kettle to boil she unbuttons her shirt and opens the fridge door. Standing in front of the open refrigerator cools her skin, quiets the heat rash across her neck and breasts. She bends into the coolness and reaches for the plate of sliced watermelon on the shelf. The kettle begins to whistle. She balances the edge of the chilled plate against her bare stomach, closes the door and turns and unplugs the kettle, the small, signal light extinguished as the power is cut off.

Porter is still asleep in the cot. Ida decides to wait until he is awake—he is lying on his back and she doesn't want to frighten him. The steam poured up into her face as she washed the knife and now her hair is clinging to her face and neck.

At first she thinks he is snoring but when she looks at him she realizes that it is the old woman sawing behind the wall.

Out of her shirt she slips. Ida sits on the edge of the cot beside Porter and eats the slices of watermelon. The juice runs down her chin and chest and into the waistband of her skirt. A drop of sweat eases down between the sharpness of her shoulder blades. Porter's chest rises and falls with a deep, even swelling. His mouth is open. His eyelids twitch.

When he sleeps his lips redden and swell, his teeth behind them are shiny and white. Ida breaks off a bit of watermelon and knocks the seeds onto the plate. She puts the piece of fruit between his lips and pushes lightly, hoping to make him accept it in his sleep. Porter's mouth is unresponsive. Ida eats the fruit herself, still watching him.

Underneath the window a passing couple begin to fight. They seem to stop directly underneath on purpose. As they raise their voices Ida hears them clearly.

"You can't make that kind of decision for me!" the man spits at his lover.

"I'm not," the woman answers. "I'm making it for me. If I force you to accept it nothing changes for you. If you force me to go through with it, everything changes."

Ida tries to tune them out. She tries to enhance the buzzing of the electrical wires. She tries to focus her hearing and send it into the telephone lines, listen in on the private sobbing of someone's mother crackling across a long distance as her daughter coos and whispers, "It will be all right. Everything will be all right."

Porter sleeps on, his dreaming soft and unrelenting as the night sky over the desert.

Ida pulls his sheet back to expose his naked length. The full, moist arrow of hair tucks darkly into the clefts of his chest and navel. His sex is quiet. His legs are apart. Ida slips down to take him in her mouth. Soft and warm and slow to rouse, Porter could be dreaming of anyone now—his mother, some actress, Ida's sister, anyone. He sleeps on, but his hips move to help her.

Her mouth gradually becoming more full, she moves her head slowly up and down, higher and lower each time. The salt of his sweat and his fever and his semen spreads across her tongue. She releases him and buries her head lower to lick at his thighs. His hands are in her hair now, he is awake.

Mutely he reaches his fingers over her jaw as she continues to stroke and kiss him. He feels his way across her cheeks and ears and back toward her face. He touches the closed orbs of her eyelids and the small bridge of her nose. He moves through her hair to grip the round back of her skull and bring her back to where she started. With her mouth completely over him again he holds her head and moves his hips urgently, quickly. When he comes he tosses his head and growls. Ida lies beside him and waits.

Finally still, Porter seems more alert, more well than he has in days. Ida props herself up on her elbow and smiles at him. She sits up and sees the knife lying with the abandoned half-moons of watermelon on the plate. She will have to wash it again.

"Are you all right?" Porter asks her.

"Yes," she says and gets up to take the plate back to the kitchen.

In the kitchen she leaves the plate on the counter and washes and wipes the knife at the sink. Porter is sitting up in bed.

She comes back to him with the knife in her hand. He sees it and silently rolls onto his stomach. Through the wall the sudden prophesizing of a late-night talk show booms. Ida bangs a closed fist against the wall and the sound immediately lowers to a dull, inconsistent murmur.

She is straddled over Porter's waist, his back is tense, waiting.

"Give me one of your hands," she demands. He twists his arm behind his back so that she can reach his hand and grip it.

Each time that she slashes him she digs her nails into his hand. Seven long red lines, she makes, across his back and then she lets him go. He is shuddering, his teeth are grinding loudly. She leaves him and walks to the bathroom.

Squeezing the flesh around the wounds, she draws his blood out easily and soaks it up with a towel. He bleeds for longer than she expected; the towel is quickly dyed an even crimson.

When the shallow cuts whiten and begin to raise she shows him the towel. He relaxes a little.

"That's the bad blood?" he says.

"That's some of the bad blood," she answers. He moves to roll over but she firmly holds him still.

"Wait a little while longer before you move," she tells him. "Try and keep your body away from your mind."

With the back of her hand she strokes his head soothingly. A breeze comes in from the window, cooling them. The traffic swishes softly far away—news trucks, ambulances, police cars, roaming silently, for the moment, without any clear prey.

It is some time before Porter can roll onto his side and Ida can finally slip out of her skirt and panties and lie on her side against him. The fever having been released, they lie closely together and wait for the night to be thinned by the morning. The old woman has disappeared. The dog has stopped barking. Ida says something before she falls asleep but Porter does not hear her.

THE
PROUD
SELENOGRAPHER

Do you believe in innocence? Not in the effect of innocence, the charming stunned expression of a foreigner, a virgin, or a child, but in the state of innocence. I wonder sometimes if the only way that an adult can ever find themselves in the state of innocence again is either by falling in love unexpectedly or by lying frozen under a general anaesthetic.

I'm not being difficult. I'm only trying to find a way to talk to you.

Perhaps it happens more often if you think of innocence as a complete lack of intention held in place for short periods of time by emotional helplessness. If you were driving your car on a rainy night and the lights of another car suddenly appeared, bearing down on you, you could kick the brakes or swerve away, but very quickly everything that could be done would be done and you would become an empty observer of your own life. And then you might be innocent.

When the café door opened just now the wind blew a white pile of napkins along the speckled blue counter toward me. A man walked in and looked around until he saw a woman sitting in the far booth, facing away from him.

She has very red hair; I expect that's how he usually locates her. She turns in her seat to look over her shoulder at him when she recognizes his footsteps. She smiles. I don't think it has been very long since they last saw each other. I think I see a brief gleam of light follow the movement of her hand but I couldn't see if it was a wedding ring. If it was, then he is not wearing the match for it. He sits down and I hear her high voice begin rushing out in a hushed little wave. He laughs and studies his menu, beginning to return her conversation only very sparely in a voice at least an octave lower than hers. My guess is that he is twenty-eight and she is twenty-six. My guess is that they have known each other a very long time and that he was once in love with her but now they are both involved with other people and the intimate inclination of their postures is half involuntary and half a joke between them.

There is another man sitting in the booth behind them with his slumped back to them. He is trying to read a book, irritated by the intrusion of their compelling voices. He sighs and puts his book down, folding a napkin in at the page that he left off at. He lifts his coffee to his mouth. I can't see his mouth. I don't know these people.

The wind is moving faster now as I walk out. It urges me not to be coy about my destination. To bend my head down, pull my coat around me and be determined.

And now I remember the first night of our marriage. It was cold like this but the wind was still. It was a different season. I waited for you in the bed. I was so wet beneath the sheets. I lay there listening to you in the bathroom, washing your face and shaving and brushing your teeth and flossing and brushing your teeth again. The bed grew deeper. I fell asleep some- how, before you were done. And when I woke up you were already inside me, your dark face over mine, your eyes empty mirrors focused on mine. And you were moving in and out of me, not making a sound, only the two parts of us touching and I reached up and covered your mouth with my hands and held onto your loose mouth, unable to make myself move beneath you, and when you started to come I felt as if something terrible had happened. Nothing could be taken back. We were never going to be the same.

Your brother said once that you were the smartest man he'd ever met but I think he didn't know you very well. I'm sure that almost no one knew that you memorized things to say to them that you had heard elsewhere about important topics. But you didn't know any of those things, not truly inside yourself.

And now I remember the second night of our marriage, when I sat myself over your lap and took you inside me and you lay still except for hands kneading hips.

"Open your eyes."

"I don't want to."

I bent my head down and kissed your mouth and took your warm bottom lip between my teeth. I pressed my chest against the soft black mat of your chest and my stomach against your stomach and I rocked gently over you, my hair a shroud over your face.

"What's wrong?"

"I don't want to come."

"How can you not want to come?"

"I just don't. Please get off me."

And now I remember the third night of our marriage, when we got drunk in our dark livingroom with our two best friends and you kissed her and he kissed me and he kissed you and after they left we went to bed and never said another word about it.

And the tenth night, when you shot yourself. Surely there was no reason. And I remember the black pool spreading beneath my hands where I held your head up and started screaming.

You were a bad husband, John. I don't love you.

The brain learns depression and it teaches the body. There are many things in the world that can trigger the acidic first flood of grief. Once those tributaries are established they fill easily and get deeper with every rain.

I wish I had gotten pregnant one of those nights. My womb feels bruised to me. I would give anything to lie in a hospital bed and split apart and drag you back into this world again.

I now have a firm plan to make love to all of your friends as soon as they are speaking to me. I hope you can hear me. I'm going to fuck them one by one, every one. And then you.

I broke all your dishes. I never liked them.

It's very hard to describe you. I can't seem to hold on to your face. It's as if everything I knew of you was transmuted into the stiff shaft of movement that hammered away inside me the first night of our marriage; hammered away until we both dissolved.

You were so tall, I could stand on your feet and still only rest my head on your chest. Your brother told me at the funeral that your mother killed herself as well. It seems like a funny thing to run in families. I guess it happens that way with salmon. You should have been the one to tell me that. You should have written me a letter or said something prophetic before you went into the bathroom that night. You should have done it when I wasn't home. Or did you want me there? Was it because you loved me so much and you felt safer to do it when I was home? Or were you really afraid? Or did you just want to hurt me?

You had such beautiful hair. So black and shiny, purple when we were walking outside in the summer. Once I knew you were dead and no one had heard me screaming I sat down very calmly beside you. I guess you have no way of knowing that. And I just held my head between my hands and looked at you. I couldn't call anybody. I didn't know what to do. My skin iced over. Your eyes filled with milky tears. And then it occurred to me to cut your hair. I ran to get the scissors. I didn't like to leave you alone like that on the bathroom floor, so vulnerable. I held your head in my lap and I carefully combed out your bangs and snipped your hair close to the skin and I put each lock, after it fell into my hand, into an envelope.

When I was a little girl I thought that a selenographer was someone who photographed the moon. I used to sit up in my room when my parents were out. I couldn't let myself go to sleep until they came home, so I filled my rocking chair with pillows and I pulled it to my window and stuffed myself into it and stared out at the pale bruised dime of the moon, listening to invisible pterodactyls, waiting for them to come home.

The first time that I saw Edvard Munch's *The Scream* we were together somewhere. I thought that the emaciated face of the screamer, so vaporously white and skull-like with his hollow eyes and lipless, stretched, open mouth, thin hands pressed to his ears, wasn't meant to be a man at all, it was the moon. And you leaned down to my ear. The floor creaked. Your breath moved my hair and you smelt soft, roasted and spongy, like your brown suede jacket and humus and you said to me that he wasn't screaming—he was reacting to hearing someone else scream.

BREATHING
IN APRIL

Madeleine's watch is broken. Depressed, sitting on the bus, she shakes her wrist beside her ear. This is a rainy April. It is always dark when she gets up. The rain coming down on her aluminum roof drowns out the clatter and spit of her ancient coffee maker.

Madeleine is writing a novel which she knows is not very good. She is pretty but skinny. Her ankles knock together when she walks. Madeleine is married, but no one has ever seen her husband close up. Occasionally, when he picks her up downtown after a movie, one of her friends sees them together, across the street.

Today she is going to the doctor. She has a fever. She is having trouble sleeping again.

Dr. Touros smiles when she comes in the door. He pats the steel examination table as if it were the sun-warmed sofa cushion beside him. Without speaking, Madeleine undresses. The redheaded nurse is there, watching, for insurance purposes. Confident hands probe her thyroid, her glands; the low drone of the doctor's questions is occasionally broken by the high buzz of her own distant answers. His touch is comfortingly invasive.

She wishes it were summer. She wishes she were horseback riding. The wide, warm body of the horse rocking her away through fields of long, yellow grass; the sun filling a hot circle on top of the round crown of her hair.

It isn't true that she is having nightmares. Her night disturbances are of a more romantic nature. She dreams of being seduced by a black bear. He scoops her up in hot, matted arms and presses his cool, wet nose between her lips. Weepy eyes burn in his solid forehead.

She wakes up pressing her legs together hard. The amber acorns of her cat's eyes glisten in the dark. The cat blinks when she rolls over and blows gently into its tiny face. Her husband does not live with her.

The doctor says that she is all right, not sick, just tired. He asks her if she couldn't get someone to cover her shifts at the restaurant for a week?

No. Everyone is busy, everyone is always busy. And she needs the money. Easter is good money, holidays always are. She buttons up her shirt crooked, flattens her brown, curly hair, pushing it through the elastic circle, pulling it tight. It's a waste of time, the doctor never tells her what she comes for. What does she come for?

Tell me I have cancer, tell me that I'm dying, I have only five days, scare me, push me, make my heart beat. Still, she is relieved. She is glad to refill the prescription for sleeping pills she will not take.

On the bus again she watches an old man standing, talking to the bus driver. She is fascinated by his refusal to appreciate the driver's rejection. As he talks he begins to shuffle his feet. His legs loosen, swinging more at the knees. His arms rock. He snaps his fingers. The driver pulls over at the next stop and addresses him loudly, for the first time, "I told you before," he says, "don't dance."

Getting off the bus early wasn't actually planned. When Madeleine looks up and sees the tall, gray and red rectangle, moving off, leaving her behind, she thinks, I should be looking for something.

On the corner across the road there is a bookshop, heavy and dusty-dry but bright. Madeleine watches a man enter the store. Brass chimes attached to the door ring as he jostles it. Madeleine decides to go and see the books.

The store is remarkably small. Shelves go all the way up to the ceiling and dirty, rubber footstools are still standing where the last person needed them. Behind the counter a round man in his early fifties leans against the wall, dangerously straining the back of his wooden chair. He is wearing slippers and a wool cardigan. The man she saw walk in from across the road is griping at him. Madeleine cannot tell if he is kidding. Something about him is familiar. Madeleine tries to get closer to hear what he is complaining about. His voice is soft, he is conscious that other people can hear him. No matter how close she gets, she can only get the sound of him and not the words. From the aggravatingly clear responses of the clerk she gathers that this man has books for sale here. He must be some sort of writer. She cannot tell if the clerk admires him but he seems to like him, or at least indulge him, letting him talk on and on. Maybe the clerk just likes his voice, Madeleine does.

She sits on a dirty stool, behind the shelf between them and her. She leans her head on the uneven row of spines and just listens to his voice. He sounds so alive, his voice moving through humorous patterns, warm and low.

The sunlight streams through the door's cut-out window, spilling into her lap. Dust hangs on the sun's arms, suspended, silver. An odd-eyed tabby exchanges glances with her from where he lies, mixed in with Canadiana, on the bottom shelf. Both of them are half asleep. Madeleine is completely relaxed. Close to the floor. Close to the pretty, round mothballs. Close to the collapsed ashes of sandalwood incense.

Madeleine starts to think about her novel. It worries her that the plot might seem a little foolish. The characters might be too odd to be sympathetic. Becoming emotionally involved with the fleshless progeny of your own writing can be dangerous, misleading.

In her novel, a woman who believes that a hand-painted, porcelain tile is her child, is set upon by the child welfare commission. Legally she had been free to claim foster parent status for the tile, but when she tries to obtain a legal adoption, believing that stability is essential to a family's psychic health, the welfare authorities intercede. In matters of adoption it is their policy that children should always go to families of similar background when possible. A very sweet Hispanic couple who can't have any tiles of their own are the compassionate antagonists in the story.

When did the voice stop? Madeleine stumbles as she stands. She sees the man from behind, slipping out the door, this time leaving the chimes quiet. Tripping over her skirt she knocks the shelves on both sides of her, hurting her knee and her shoulder. The angry cat is sent running. The clerk barely smiles and does not sit up as she rushes past him, into the street.

It's not that she means to follow him. She is not curious about him, there isn't anything she wants to ask him for. In the sun she can see that he is lean, but not tall. He has black hair, black shoes, and a thick black moustache. He is carrying a pale pine briefcase which looks like an old paint box. He walks self-consciously with the casual aggression of someone who is enjoying himself but is prepared not to.

Suddenly Madeleine feels like playing. Following is a game. This is just like *Death in Venice*. She is the lurid, old Aschenbach, stumbling, besotted through the streets after the shining, golden figure of Tadzio. Every other step she skips, dodging villainous gondoliers and the giggling, dark fingers of the plague. It is not important how little she resembles the old man, or how unlike the cherub Tadzio this man is. Madeleine does not care for characteristics, only for essence.

"I have to get some papers and then I'm going to the beach."

He has turned and spoken directly to her. The brick building they stand in front of must contain his apartment. He holds the door open but she stays, silent on the street until he shrugs and goes in. He has thrown her off guard, switched the game. She tries to see which window is his. She does not know whether to stay or to run. At least she has been practical enough not to go up to a strange man's room. When he comes out again he looks directly at her and smiles. She smiles back, relieved to be taken by instinct.

"I'll walk you," he says. She follows him, uncertain, wondering how this will turn into a new game. In the alleys that take them there are crusty tires and the rusted, gory entrails of cars and dishwashers. He points to a stain as they step past it. "Blood," he says.

Concrete walls block out any landmarks. Madeleine keeps looking up at the sky, feeling somehow that they might be underground.

It is a ridiculously clean transition from city to beach. The walls stop and the gravel gives way to sand without ever the one scoring the other. Over the beach, gulls reel, skimming an invisible line overhead, defining the territory as particular, contained.

"Give me your shoes." He bends over and lifts up her feet, freeing them, first left then right. He hurries her across the sand, the hot sand, to the slick outcrop of rocks, a short staircase at the edge of the foaming water.

When they are sitting there, side by side, clapping the soles of their shoes together absently, he tells her, "I can only stay a few minutes, I'm going to see my son."

She looks at him.

"Can you breathe under water?" she asks, surprised.

"Yes," he says, "I have gills, but you can't see them, they go too deep."

He moves his hair aside to show her the smooth side of his neck. She touches the side of his neck lightly. He lowers his head to encourage her to touch the back of his neck as well.

"You don't have to stay here, you know," he mumbles contentedly into his chest. "You can, but you don't have to." Suddenly she is jealous that he has a son, someone to go to, under the water.

"Do you think that a fish can love a bird?" she asks him, turning her face to be washed by the spray off the lake.

He sits up straight and answers, "It's not very practical. Certain birds eat certain fish and certain fish have even been known to eat certain birds. But I suppose that given the patience of a bird who may only rarely catch a glimpse of the fish by accident, swimming underneath, and given the endurance of a fish willing to breathe the uncivilized, bald air in order to call out to the bird, given that a certain unusual loyalty would be required for such a relationship, it is possible that some sort of friendship could occur."

What a funny thing to say, she thinks, what an odd subject.

He stands up. He holds his briefcase over his head as he walks into the water which swallows him gently and completely without even the round scar of a ripple.

At home Madeleine watches the cream unwinding, transforming her coffee. Later, getting ready for bed, she puts aside her toothbrush and slips out of her pyjama top. Turning around and looking over her shoulder she studies the soft, sloping white of her back in the mirror.

GEORGE LOVES ODETTE

Odette is sitting in Commerce Court eating her modest lunch. She chews slowly and reads the book that is resting in her lap. A tall aboriginal man with long, gray streaked hair walks hesitantly up to her. When she glances up he says, "Can you spare a dollar for a sandwich?" She looks quickly down again without answering. He continues to stand in front of her. She can see his legs trembling inside the thin fabric of his pants. She senses him moving and she looks up. The people around her gasp. He is holding a gun to his ear. He looks into Odette's eyes.

"I'm a good man," he says. "I'm an educated man."

And he shoots himself. For a few seconds he remains standing, startled, and then he crumbles at her feet.

She is late for work. When she steps into the studio she leans against the wall and slides down to the floor and pulls her shoes off.

George comes around the corner with his Polaroid camera in one hand and a tape measure in the other.

"Take a picture of my head," he says.

"What?"

"Take a head shot of me, take a picture of my face. Come on, Odette."

He thrusts the camera into her hand, straightens up and smiles wildly. Obligingly, she photographs him. She pulls the black square to make it roll out faster and shakes it to help it dry.

George is pulling the tape measure around his head, apparently measuring his skull. Odette watches him quietly.

"George," she says, "don't call me Odette. My name is Carolyn." He looks at her and smiles.

"Carolyn's not a good name for an artist's model. Odette suits you better."

She shakes her head and folds her arms across her chest.

"I don't care. My name is Carolyn."

He puts the tape measure down and cocks his head.

"I tell you what, we'll spell it c-a-r-o-l-y-n but we'll pronounce it Odette, OK?"

She looks down at the Polaroid. George's face is beginning to emerge from the gray, photographic milk.

"Here you go," she says, and hands it to him. She pulls her book out of her pocket and tries to find the page she left off at. When she finds it, it is wrinkled and spattered dark brown.

Glancing at the cover George shakes his head.

"Odette, why can't you read trashy novels?" His voice is wheedling. "I would like you better if you read trashy, romantic, historical novels."

She doesn't respond. She just curls herself into a fetal position on the floor and continues to read. He steps behind her and crouches. He puts a hand on her shoulder and shakes her lightly.

"Hey, why are you still dressed? What time is it? It's four o'clock already, we have to get started." She doesn't respond. He falls behind her and lying on his side he gathers her against him and pushes his face through her hair to her ear.

"Odette, Odette, Odette, something's up, tell me." But she doesn't answer him.

"Look at my teeth. They're all stained and crooked. These aren't my teeth. All I need are the dental records to prove it."

Odette stands on her toes to look at his teeth.

"Your teeth are ugly, but your teeth were always ugly. You just never noticed before."

He pushes her away and says sadly, "Yes, but they were my teeth. It was my ugly."

Odette turns around and walks away from him.

"George, if someone replaced your head you'd die, believe me."

He regards her suspiciously.

"Are you a doctor? Tell me, Odette, what do you know about transplants? About immunosuppressant drugs?"

He stares into his coffee. Swishing it around and around in its heavy clay mug.

"I promise," she answers wearily, stretching her arms up over her head as she speaks, "if I ever cut your head off, I won't give you another one."

The room is cold because the studio windows are open to the night air. Odette is sitting naked on top of a four-foot pyramid of orange crates, her legs crossed, her arms wrapped around herself for warmth. Her teeth are beginning to hurt from chattering. The curtains billow in with the wind.

George is supposed to be sketching but he is poring over the head shots that he was able to find of himself, taken over the last few years.

"You know, it probably isn't a bad idea for you to take a head shot of me every day, even if it does turn out to be my head. After I'm dead you can put together an animated film of me aging."

Odette turns her head and looks out the window at the apartment building across the street. In the window parallel to hers a young boy, maybe ten or eleven, blond and fragile looking, is standing, staring at her. She cannot see what he is doing with his hands. When their eyes meet he moves to the side, behind the curtain so that she cannot see him any longer.

"George, I'm cold," she says.

He looks up from his desk at her and his pupils dilate. He sees her trying to control her shaking. He sees that her lips and knuckles are beginning to edge blue. He opens a drawer and takes out the camera. He lifts it to his eye and she is stunned by the flash and the sudden mechanical whir.

They are lying together in bed. Their bodies shine with the last bits of light left from the day.

"It is cold," he says with real wonder.

Odette rolls onto her back and stares at the paint bubbled on the damaged ceiling. George crawls up against her and throws one arm and one leg across her body to reel her back into him.

"Do you have any brothers or sisters?" he asks. She is counting to a thousand in her head.

"I have an older brother. He's in school in B.C. He's going to be an architect."

George stops her by rolling on top of her and kissing her mouth. He smoothes her hair away from her face and stares at her. He measures the length and width of her small face underneath his hand.

"I was hoping you had sisters. I had this image of three little Odettes, the oldest one nine, another one eight, and the youngest only six." She stares back at him, her eyes crossing because he is so close.

"Why do you want me to have sisters?" she says. "So that you can have more models lined up when I'm too old for you?"

He laughs and bends to whisper in her ear, "No, Odette. I want to know what you looked like before I met you. I want to watch you turn into a woman over and over again."

She rolls onto her stomach knocking him off of her as she turns. She bunches up the pillow against her face. She bites the inside of her cheek until it bleeds. He takes this opportunity to slip inside of her and begin again.

In the middle of the night he sits up straight in bed and screams as if all of his internal organs are twisting themselves inside out. She covers his mouth, but he continues to scream.

"George, what are you dreaming?"

"This is not my head," he says. "These are not my dreams. I am thinking things that I have never thought before."

In the morning she lets him sleep. She sits at his desk and pores over the Polaroids that he has taken of her recently, her toast in one hand, her coffee in the other. She does not know that he is around the corner watching her look at herself.

Odette, he asks himself, would you still pose for me if I weren't paying you?

He looks at her again and sees himself sitting at his desk. The absolute nakedness, the absolute feminine vanity of his infinite white skin seeing itself, seeing the light hitting it. He steps back and imagines that he is a bullet aimed at Odette, struggling toward Odette through this glance.

"Odette, would you still pose for me if I weren't paying you?" She looks over to see him lying on the floor by the corner.

"No," she says. She cannot understand the question.

"Would you still be sleeping with me?"

"You don't pay me to sleep with you," she says, and turns back to the pictures as if he has been easily dismissed.

"I pay you to come here and that's one of the things that you do when you come here." George is beginning to sound tortured. He is pushing his body toward her along the floor with his legs.

"George, if you want me to pose, I will pose. If you want to fuck, I will fuck. But for God's sake get off the floor. You're making me nervous."

George stands up and stares at her. She ignores him.

"A person can live within another person's head," he begins to yell. "Can migrate into new patterns of thought, can incorporate someone else's memories into their own fascination with themselves, but when you take their arms and legs and heart as well, they have to die. They have no choice."

Odette throws the scalding mug of coffee at him, picks up the photographs of her and leaves, slamming the apartment door behind her. George rushes to the window and calls after her as she runs down the street, "Odette! Odette! Carolyn!"

For two weeks he is calm. He calls her at night and whispers all of his memories of her over the phone: the things she wears, the way she sleeps. He makes outlandish promises concerning vacations, time away together, some place warm. He manages to convince her to come back. He gives her the cheque when she comes in the door. He photographs her with her clothes on. He brings her coffee and even leaves the windows closed, the curtains drawn.

On the first day that she agrees to undress for him again he places a chair in the centre of the room for her, opens the curtains and busily gathers his pencils and papers. She is good for me, he thinks. Everything about her makes sense as long as she is actually here.

"Odette," he says without looking up from the heavy paper and charcoal, "tell me a secret."

"Don't be stupid, George. A secret is something you don't tell anybody."

"You don't have any, do you?" he says and smiles at her warmly. "You're so innocent you could smuggle cocaine across the border cupped in your hands and nobody would ever stop you." Outside the window a man in a cherry picker is working on the electrical lines for the building. Because it is day and the light shines on the windows he cannot see Odette, sitting naked only a few feet away from him.

"I have secrets," she tells him disdainfully, and shifts her legs, watching the cherry picker carefully, unsure of her protection.

"Tell me then," he says and stops his drawing of her.

"I can't." She is unnerved by his attention being directed under her skin. The man in the cherry picker is very close to the window. She thinks to herself, if his shadow falls across the window he'll be able to see through me.

"You keep a secret for a certain length of time and then you can't tell it anymore."

George lays his pencil on the floor and it rolls away. He walks over to Odette, sitting in her wooden chair in the middle of the wooden floor of the huge white room. He falls on his knees in front of her and puts his arms around her waist and his face into her lap. She runs her hand through his hair.

She leans her body over him but she does not know how to comfort him.

"He's going to meet you on the street." He speaks to her belly. "He's going to look at you and know everything that I know about you. He'll see you with your blouse open at the front, with your dress pushed up to your waist, with your long skirt flipped across your back. He's going to see you and he's going to look around in my head and figure out where I live and come here and kill me."

George is shaving in the bathroom. Odette has not arrived yet. As he holds the skin of his cheek taut and pulls the razor along it he becomes increasingly irritated by having to continue caring for a face that no longer belongs to him. He puts the razor aside and looks at his shoulders and chest. He runs his hand over his stomach. He leans in close to the mirror to examine his neck. He hurries into the studio to find something. When he returns to the bathroom he has a red marker in his hand. He wipes the area around the base of his neck dry with a towel and taking the cap off of the marker he begins to draw a line around the precise border between him and the other.

The door bangs open and Odette rushes in. She sees the empty studio and walks immediately to the bedroom. George comes out of the bathroom and walks into the bedroom behind her.

"George," she laughs as she turns around and bumps into him. She puts her hands on top of his shoulders and jumps up, grabbing him around the waist with her legs so that he can hold her there. He holds her wrapped around him and listens.

"I've found him, George. He lives across the street. I saw him watching us through the window once, but I didn't know until today that he was the one. It's not even a man wearing your head, George, it's just a little boy. It should be easy to get it back from him!"

"Are you sure?" George asks her, becoming infected by her excitement. "How could you tell?" He carries her across the room and deposits her on the bed. They lie facing each other.

"I was sitting on a bench outside reading my book before I came up and I heard someone bouncing a basketball on the sidewalk beside me. I looked up and there he was, standing beside me looking at me, this blond, thin-faced boy. He just kept looking at me so boldly that I got nervous. He was bouncing his ball and rolling his eyes over me the way you do when you are trying to figure out what position to put me into before you draw me. And then I remembered seeing him before. He lives in the apartment across from you. He stands at the window and looks at me while you draw. I realize now that you don't look at me when you draw anymore, but while you are drawing, he is looking."

George is listening intently, nodding his head along with each point.

"And then I asked him what his name was and he just kept bouncing that ball and staring. I asked him again, 'What's your name?" and he kept staring and bouncing. And then he sneered at me, 'I know your name.' And I said, 'all right, what's my name?' and he paused and then he said, 'It's either Carolyn or Odette.'"

George leans up on his elbow and stares into her eyes.

"It's him. We've got to catch him."

It takes them two days to build the cage. They tear apart all the orange crates and nail them together with long cross beams made out of wood that George steals at night from a new housing development a few blocks away. The crates make up the top and bottom of the cage and the beams nailed to the top and bottom form bars around the side. The door is still a hole in the cage. George plans to tear off the bathroom door and nail it over the hole once they have the boy.

"Odette, stand in the cage."

Odette looks at George. "But, George, I'm helping you."

George takes the two steps that it takes to stand against her. He leans down to brush her hair off of her shoulder and whisper in her ear, "Look out the window." Odette looks over George's shoulder out the window and sees the boy standing half-hidden behind a curtain, watching.

She steps into the cage, ducking because it is not tall enough for her to stand.

"You are such a good girl," George croons. "Now take off your clothes."

Odette unzips her jeans and sits on the floor of the cage to pull them off. She pulls her sweater over her head and sits there in her bra and panties looking at George.

"He's seen you before," he says. So she finishes undressing and George reaches through the bars and pulls her clothing out.

"It's not going to work, George. He can see the door, he knows I can get out again." George stands up and stretches his arms out to grip the sides of the cage and shake it.

"OK, you're right. Come and stand just outside the doorway," he tells her. She stands in front of the doorway and covers her head when George tells her to. He walks around to the other side of the cage and pushes it so that it falls over her, knocking her to the ground and trapping her inside. George runs to his desk to get the camera and steps around the cage taking pictures of Odette as she gets up, shakes her head and gathers her legs against her chest.

"I hurt my back. Let me out."

But George is getting a hammer and nails from his desk and striding back to busily begin nailing the sides of the cage to the floor.

"George, I hurt my back. Let me out. He's not going to come over here and jump in a cage with me while you're here. And if you nail it down, how can he get in?"

"He's little. He can slip through the bars."

"If he can slip in then he can slip back out again. Let me out." She looks at him through the slats. "But, George," she says, "I'm helping you."

He is standing pressed up against the cage with his arms wrapped around one side. She looks around to the window and sees the boy now standing in full view in the middle of the window, pressing himself against the glass in imitation of George, holding onto the window frame.

"I'm cold," she says.

It is dark. She feels the tiny, sharp stabs of splinters working their way deeper into her every time she moves. She stares out at the hollow, empty dark of the boy's window. She sits in the corner holding herself for warmth. Eventually she falls asleep sitting up, leaning against the cheap, citrus-scented wood.

When she sleeps she dreams she is lying on a beach listening to the water rushing in and out over the sand. She can feel George's body beside her and his low voice whispering in her ear asking her what she is dreaming.

"I'm dreaming that I am on an operating table," she tells him. "There's a huge light shining down on me and people around the table moving around, whispering. I'm dreaming that a man with a cold, deep voice leans close to my ear and whispers to me, 'What-is-in-your-heart?'

"'I don't know, I don't know,' I say. And then I feel a scalpel pressing at the base of my throat, sliding down into my chest, and a hand reaching in and pulling something out. From somewhere over my head I hear someone press the play button on an old portable tape recorder, and I hear our voices recorded over the phone, me saying: 'I hate you, I hate you so much I could spit.' You saying: 'That's all right. Tell me more.'"